Simon Grave
and the
Girl with the
Crab Tattoo

Len Boswell

Black Rose Writing | Texas

ISBN: 978-1-68513-461-7
PUBLISHED BY BLACK ROSE WRITING
www.blackrosewriting.com

Printed in the United States of America
Suggested Retail Price (SRP) $19.95

Simon Grave and the Girl with the Crab Tattoo is printed in Palatino Linotype

Other books by Len Boswell

Fantasies:
Barnum's Angel
The Barnacle's Son
The Cave of the Six Arrows
The Fool's Gambit

Simon Grave Mysteries:
A Grave Misunderstanding
Simon Grave and the Curious Incident of the Cat in the Daytime
Simon Grave and the Drone of the Basque Orvilles
Simon Grave and the Sons of Irony
Simon Grave and the School of Casual Invisibility
Simon Grave and the Wrath of Grapes
Simon Grave and the Girl with the Crab Tattoo

Other Mysteries:
Flicker: A Paranormal Mystery
Skeleton: A Bare Bones Mystery
Penelope Goodlove's Invisible Detective Agency: The Elephant Who Cried Wolf

Novellas:
LIQ: The Quality of Mercy

Memoirs:
Santa Takes a Tumble
Unboxing Raymond

Nonfiction:
The Leadership Secrets of Squirrels
Stick Figures: The Life and Art of Len Boswell

Check them out here: https://www.lenboswellauthor.com

To all I love without condition
To all I love without omission

Never doubt

"Everything that happens once can never happen again. But everything that happens twice will surely happen a third time."
—Paulo Coelho, *The Alchemist*

kis·met *noun* destiny; fate.
"What chance did I stand against kismet?"

Simon Grave

and the
Girl with the
Crab Tattoo

1

It was the kind of sunrise you hear about but rarely see, the colors of dawn reflected not along the horizon but higher, on the underbelly of a bank of high, roiling clouds scudding across the sky above Crab Cove and the Greater Crabopolis, the kind of clouds that could easily hide the sleek gray mass of a mother ship far, far from its home planet.

But Detective Simon Grave knew no mother ship would be descending from the clouds. It would be a simple shuttle returning from the Mars Colony, with a very special passenger, Wanda Orville, who had fled to Mars after murdering her husband, Frank, two years ago. She would be escorted by an officer of the Mars Security Force, who would turn her over to the Crab Cove Police upon arrival.

The terminal was bustling, as it always did on the arrival or departure of a shuttle. Arnold Schwarzenegger simdroids scurried about, some pushing luggage carts toward the "I'm Back!" arrival gate, and some checking in passengers at the "I'll Be Back!" gate.

Grave and Sergeant Blunt sat in the front row of the arrival seating area, crossing and uncrossing their legs, folding and unfolding their arms across their chests, and shaking their heads and checking their watches in synchronous impatience. Two Officer Larry simdroids, by contrast, stood motionless, waiting patiently for orders.

And then she appeared, along with a female officer who looked too young for the job.

Wanda Orville seemed even more beautiful than Grave remembered, from her blond hair to her blue eyes to her alluring figure to her red-striped prison garb to the way she spat at him on first sight.

"Ah," said Grave, "I see you remember me."

Wanda sneered at him, which as sneers go, was also beautiful. "You bastard!"

"Nice to see you, too, Wanda." He turned to the police escort. "And you would be?"

The escort seemed more girl than woman. She was short and thin, like Detective Snoot, but with close-cropped red hair and eyes of disconcertingly different colors, one brown, the other violet. A red salamander tattoo peeked out from behind her collar. She was dressed in the traditional uniform of the Mars Security Force: gold-trimmed red shirt and trousers, with black knee-high boots. The effect was more lion tamer than police officer. Overall, when it came to beauty, she was no Wanda Orville, but there was something there, something hidden behind her stern, no-nonsense manner, a strident beauty waiting for you to dare it to come out. And then, by god, you'd have your hands full.

She extended her hand and shook Grave's with a crunching intensity he wasn't expecting. "Salamander, Kismet Salamander." She pointed to the bars on her collar. "Detective first class."

Grave pulled his hand away as soon as he was able, and tried not to grimace as much as he knew he was. "I'm Detective Simon Grave, and this is my partner, Sergeant Blunt. Pleased to meet you, detective."

"Me, too," said Blunt.

Salamander squinted at him. "You're almost not there, you know. I can barely see you."

Blunt sighed. "Yes, I get that a lot."

"We could use you on Mars. They'd think you were a phantom in the whirling dust."

Blunt attempted a chuckle. "No, thank you. I have enough trouble making myself present here on Earth."

Salamander gave Blunt a nod. "I hear you." She turned back to Grave. "I have papers you'll need to sign."

"Of course, but first things first." He turned to the Officer Larrys. "Take Wanda to the station and turn her over to Captain Morgan."

The Officer Larrys wasted no time, grabbing Wanda by each arm and almost dragging her away, Wanda trying her best to kick at them. "Bastards!"

Grave gave her a little wave. "Buh-bye."

Salamander just smirked. "She's been like that the whole time. A right pain in the arse is what she is."

"I believe it," said Grave. "Now, as to the papers."

"Oh, yes." She reached into her back pocket and produced a document and a pen. "Here you go."

Grave started to take the papers, but his personal drone, Barry, suddenly zoomed into the waiting area, shouting his name. "Grave, Grave, Grave!"

"What is it?"

"A body. They've found a body in the town square. Morgan wants you there right away."

"Tell him we're on our way." He turned to Salamander, grabbed the document, and signed it, shoving it back into her hands. "Thank you for your service. Have a safe trip back."

And then he turned, grabbed Blunt by the arm, and ran for the exit.

2

Grave could see the Larrys from a block away as they cordoned off a small area near the front window of the Skunk 'n Donuts. And they could hear his Austin Healy Sprite as it roared down the street, its radio blasting out gospel music full volume, the sound shaking the leaves on the trees in the town square.

Grave zipped into a parking space across the street and turned off the engine, the sound of the radio dying quickly.

"You know," said Blunt, pulling out his earplugs, "I think I'm beginning to like this music. It's so soulful."

"Well, that's the point," said Grave. "Come on, if I'm not mistaken, Polk is already here."

"And the captain," said Blunt, pointing at Captain Henry Morgan, who was bent over at the waist, watching Polk poke at what looked like the body of a young woman.

Grave and Blunt managed to extract themselves from the Sprite's small cabin and walked over to the crime scene.

"We're here," said Grave to Captain Morgan.

"No kidding," said Morgan. "We sort of heard you coming."

Grave shrugged. "Right, so what do we have?"

"Young woman. Seems to have been dumped here, naked as a jaybird."

"Has Polk established cause and time of death?"

Polk, who had been on his knees, examining the body, stood up to his full height, which was not much higher than a fireplug. "You know, I'm right here. You could ask me."

"Didn't want to interrupt."

"So the answer is no, not yet, but she certainly died before dawn. Some guy walking his dog discovered it at 5:37, or at least that's what he said."

"So definitely before dawn?"

"Yes, body temperature suggests 2:00 a.m. or so, but the body would have been protected from the wind here, so maybe earlier."

"This Skunk 'n Donuts closes at midnight, so it would have been after that for sure. A lot of people here, even that late."

"Well, there's your window then," said Polk. He turned to Captain Morgan. "If it's okay with you, I'll take her back to the morgue now. Should have more information for you later today."

"That's fine," said Morgan. "The sooner the better."

"Wait a second," said Grave. "I'd like to take a quick look at the body."

Morgan started to reply, but the sound of an approaching hovercycle caught his attention. "What do we have here?"

The hovercycle pulled up next to Morgan and stopped. A young woman dressed in a strange red uniform pulled off her helmet and climbed off, extending her hand to Captain Morgan, who was reluctant to offer it. "I'm Kismet Salamander, Detective First Class, Mars Security Force. I see you need help."

Captain Morgan, who was a master at befuddlement, reached into his library of befuddlement responses and managed to stammer, "Wha-what?"

Grave interrupted. "The MSF escort for Wanda Orville. Brought her in this morning."

Morgan blinked twice, the information clicking into place. "Oh, I see."

Salamander pushed past him. "And if you don't mind, I'll just have a look at the body."

Morgan moved aside, thinking to object, but saying nothing.

Salamander slipped on latex gloves and turned the body over. "Ah, here we go. A tattoo. Of a crab. On her inner thigh here. Fresh. Newly inked." She pulled off her gloves and put them in her pocket. "So, looks like the place to start is every tattoo parlor in this town."

She moved past Morgan and got back on her hovercycle. "I've arranged for accommodations at the Crab Claw Inn. I'll check in and then meet you at the station in twenty minutes. We need to get this investigation going as soon as possible."

She put on her helmet, then turned back to Morgan. "We'll need a list of the parlors, so get someone started on that."

And with that, she started up the hovercycle and sped away.

Morgan looked at Grave. Grave looked at Morgan. Blunt looked at Morgan. Polk looked at Grave. Grave looked at Polk. Morgan looked at Polk. Polk looked at Blunt.

They all seemed to have the same reaction. "What the—"

3

Grave and Blunt sat opposite Captain Morgan in his glassed-in office, the squad room outside the office buzzing dolefully as it always did on Monday mornings, when the coffee was bad and the donuts were missing.

"I'm befuddled," said Morgan. "Who is this woman?"

"I'm baffled," said Grave. "Why does she think she can help with our investigation?"

"I'm both baffled and befuddled," said Blunt. "But I'm also amused—and *intrigued*. She went straight for that tattoo and kick-started the investigation. She seems to have skills, so I think we should hear her out."

Morgan grunted, as he always did when he was indecisive. "Maybe."

"Maybe?" said Grave. "You can't be serious. There hasn't been a murder at the Mars Colony—*ever*. How is she going to help?"

Captain Morgan was about to grunt, as he always did when he was challenged, but he was stopped by an uproar in the squad room. People were cheering with a gusto that usually only came with an announcement of pay raises or an unexpected holiday.

"What the—" said Morgan, standing to get a better look.

It was that Martian woman, Kismet Salamander, carrying two large boxes of donuts and a large thermos of coffee from Skunk 'n Donuts. She let two Officer Larrys unburden her, and then marched straight for Morgan's office, bursting in without so much as a knock. "Quite a morning," she said with a smile. She pointed back toward the squad room. "Thought you should have some refreshment before we begin. Donuts and coffee." She turned to Grave. "Wanda said you preferred chocolate donuts, so there's two dozen of them."

Grave was stunned, and thankful, and a little giddy. "Chocolate? Really?"

"Yes, but by the looks of it, they're disappearing fast."

Grave could see she was right. Everyone in the squad room seemed to be waving chocolate donuts in the air. He turned to Morgan. "Sir?"

"Go on," said Morgan. "You too, Blunt. Let me have a little talk with Detective, um, Salamander."

Grave and Blunt seemed to evaporate, there one second and gone the next.

Salamander watched him go. "He's a strange man, isn't he?"

"At times," said Morgan.

"You know, you guys are legends on Mars, which is part of why I'm here."

"Yes, let's get to that. Why on Earth are you here? I mean other than escorting our fugitive."

"You don't know?"

Morgan shrugged. "No. Know what?"

Salamander reached into her pocket, pulled out a folded document, and handed it to Captain Morgan.

Morgan opened it. "A proclamation?"

"Yes, announcing that the Mars Colony and Crab Cove are now declared sister cities. See, it's signed by the mayor of the colony and your mayor, too."

"I see that, but what does that have to do with you, um, being here."

"As part of our new relationship, each city agrees to exchange staff at all levels, including the police forces."

"I don't see that anywhere in this document, and the mayor has said nothing to me."

Salamander looked down at Morgan's foot-high inbox and smiled. "Um . . . are you sure?"

Morgan sighed. She was probably absolutely right, but he didn't want to sort through the inbox in front of her. It would just be too embarrassing. "No, actually, so let's assume you're right about this whole thing. What are the details of this, um, *arrangement?*"

"I am to spend a month with you, participating fully in any and all investigations so that I might learn new techniques for possible adoption and application on Mars."

"I see, and this exchange business. Am I hearing you right that we are to send someone to Mars?"

"Indeed, and today, on this evening's shuttle flight."

Morgan shook his head and grunted, as he always did when quick action was required. "Oh, my."

4

Grave had managed to stuff three chocolate donuts into his mouth before Captain Morgan emerged from his office with Kismet Salamander. Both were smiling, which didn't make sense to Grave. Morgan was supposed to send her on her way. Nothing to do here. Goodbye and good luck. But all Morgan was doing was raising his arms.

"Attention, everyone." He waited a few seconds. "May I have your attention, please?"

Finally, everyone settled down.

"I have an announcement to make. It seems our esteemed new mayor, Tiffany Tally—may she fund us fully this year—has decided to make Crab Cove a sister city to the Mars Colony. I'm not sure of all the ins and outs of this—yet—but one of the things that comes along with sisterhood is an exchange of staff." He nodded toward Salamander. "This is Kismet Salamander, Detective First Class in the Mars Security Force." He motioned her to step forward. "Come on, don't be shy. Tell us a little bit about yourself."

Salamander turned as red as the salamander tattoo on her neck and shook her head. "No."

"Come on, Kiz."

"No," she said, looking at the floor, "and don't call me Kiz."

Morgan puffed out his cheeks. "Very well, no problem. Let me just read a bit from the papers provided by the mayor of the Mars Colony."

He pulled out his reading glasses and balanced them on the end of his nose. "Here's what it says."

Office of the Mayor
Mars Colony
June 5, 2055

Dear Mayor Tally:

It is my honor to present to you our representative from the Mars Colony, Detective Kismet Salamander, of our Mars Security Force. She was chosen over all others for two reasons. First, she is, at 18, the youngest recipient of our highest security award, the Red Salamander Award, which recognizes courageous acts in defending the Colony. In this case, Salamander, with no thought for her safety and against great odds, single-handedly took down a drug and oxygen ring on the night of October 4, 2054, killing three and wounding seven, while stopping the transport of drugs and oxygen valued at seven billion Martian Marks, which I believe converts to $600 million.

Second, and perhaps most important, she is the first Martian, born to original colonists Alexander and Ethel Salamander in 2036, a year after their arrival on Mars.

It is my hope that Kismet (don't call her Kiz) will learn valuable new techniques that she can bring back to us here on Mars, as well as share our methods with your officers.

Sincerely,

Esmeralda Flitt, Mayor

Captain Morgan dropped the letter to his side, and turned to Salamander. "Very impressive, Salamander. We'll do everything we can to make your time with us valuable to you and the Mars Colony."

Salamander nodded and looked away.

Morgan turned back to the assembled staff. "Now, all detectives into the conference room, please. We have things to discuss. The rest of you get back to work—or your donuts."

5

Salamander sat in the corner of the conference room, trying hard not to participate in the discussion about who should be sent to Mars. She just wanted to observe and perhaps learn a little bit about each one of them.

First there was the gruff and curmudgeonly Captain Morgan, who overflowed his chair, the buttons on his overstuffed uniform threatening to shoot across the room. He was a man of grunts and moans, and was not one to hide his emotions. She sensed that she could trust what he said, whatever that might be.

Detective Grave was intriguing, from his rumpled gray suit to his slicked back black hair, to the way he seemed to balance confidence and incompetence when he moved and spoke. He didn't seem as smart as she was led to believe by his case success rate, which was legendary on Mars. The ring of chocolate icing around his mouth didn't give her a feeling of confidence about him, either. And he kept glancing over at Detective Polly Loblolly in a way far less than professional. Were they a couple?

Loblolly was a blond bombshell, and knew it. But she also seemed extremely bright and carried herself with as much self-confidence as allure. She could be valuable on Mars, but also a serious distraction, for men and women alike. From the way she rolled her eyes at Detective Snoot as the captain made his dubious points, Salamander could tell they must be partners.

Snoot herself seemed to be much like Salamander, in physique and demeanor. And there was something of the rebel in her that would be a problem on Mars, where strict discipline was not just required, but a matter of life and death. One false move could be her death, or worse, the death of the entire colony.

Sergeant Blunt was perhaps the most intriguing of all. His ability to be there and not be there seemed impossible, but Salamander had heard stories of such people, including the story of his daughter, who could appear and disappear at will. Salamander was jealous of that skill and hoped Blunt or his daughter could teach her how to do it. The ability to sneak up on a criminal would be wonderful.

And then there was that simdroid, Detective Freeman, who was a dead ringer for late actor Morgan Freeman. He was dressed all in white and kept referring to himself in the third person as "God." If it came down to him going to Mars, Salamander would strenuously object. Mars wanted a human, not an AI-assembled facsimile.

The same was true for Detective Charlize Theron and her partner, Doctor Smithers-Watson. Cute as they were pretending to be Sherlock Holmes and Doctor Watson, they were still simdroids, and just not right for the job.

And when she thought about it, they were all a bit odd, as was everything she had encountered so far on Earth, from its heavy gravity, to the thick air, to the personal drones that followed everyone around, to the horrible smells. *Why do these people smell so bad?*

The conversation was not going well. No one but God wanted to go. Blunt balked because he was married, which was a valid excuse, but Grave and the others just said various versions of, "Gee, I really would rather not go."

Captain Morgan had groaned, grunted, and moaned throughout the discussion, and seemed to have reached a level of frustration that was about to explode.

"Listen," he said "Someone has got to go, so if no one volunteers, I'll have to pick one. Even if it means eenie-meanie-miney-mo."

"I said I'd go," said God, standing. "No problem."

Morgan rolled his eyes. "And I told you *no*. They want a human being, not a simdroid god."

God sat back down. "Whatever."

Morgan looked around the room once more. "Still no volunteers?"

Everyone looked up, down, or generally away from his stare.

"Very well," he said, raising his hand and pointing at them. "Eenie, meanie—"

There was a sudden rapping at the door.

"Yes?" said Morgan.

"It's me, sir," said a woman's voice. "Tilda Must. May I come in?"

Salamander couldn't believe in the change in demeanor of everyone in the room. The whole room brightened, with Grave and Morgan suppressing giggles.

"Oh, yes, please come in, Retective Must."

She stuck her head in. "Oh, I didn't realize I was interrupting anything. It's just about the post-investigation reports. They're seriously late, so I'd like to talk to you about them at some point."

"No worries, Tilda," said Morgan. "Everyone was just leaving, so your timing is perfect. More to the point, I have just learned of a wonderful opportunity for you, so come in, come in."

He turned to the others. "Thank you for your input. Let's take a ten-minute break, and then discuss the case."

Everyone started to leave as quickly as they could.

"Not you, Salamander. I'd like you to meet our Retective Must, who's responsible for keeping us on our toes, critically analyzing our every move on each and every investigation."

He turned to Must. "This is Detective Kismet Salamander. She's a Martian."

Must blinked, then smiled. "Oh, how interesting. I've always wanted to go to Mars, but my duties here are so demanding. I swear, the days aren't long enough. Right, captain?"

Morgan smiled. "Yes, yes, but let's see if we can lighten your load."

Must frowned. "What?"

"Sit down, Tilda, sit down. As I said, I think I have a great opportunity for you, one that I'm sure will make you happy and the rest of us proud."

Maintaining a frown was never a problem for Tilda Must, so she carried it with her as she slid slowly into a chair next to Morgan. "Sir?"

6

Morgan looked at his watch. "Polk won't have any results for us until this afternoon, but I thought we could at least begin. We have a body. A woman. A woman with a crab tattoo . . ."

"A fresh crab tattoo," said Salamander. "Black. A simple tribal design a tourist might get. And small. And cheap, so she didn't want to spend any money. Or didn't have much money to begin with. Or just wanted something small. And it's her only tattoo. She's a beginner."

"Um, yes," said Morgan.

"Oh, and its placement, on the inner right thigh, high up, suggests she didn't want many people to see it."

Morgan interrupted. "But not so high that it would be covered by a bikini. And she did have bikini tan lines."

Salamander nodded at him. "Very good, captain. What else?"

"She's young," said Grave. "I'd guess seventeen."

"And colors her hair," said Blunt.

"What about her body?" said Charlize. "Was she fat, thin, athletic?"

"Athletic, very athletic," said Salamander. "And well endowed, a real beauty."

"Speaking of that," said Blunt. "I noticed how muscular she was. Not weight-lifter, body-builder muscular, but the kind of muscular that comes with sports. Volleyball, perhaps."

"No," said Salamander. "Tennis. Her right forearm was way bigger than her left."

"And there's a tournament in town," said Grave. "At the Crab Cove Country Club. Already in the quarter finals."

Salamander held up a hand. "Wait, wait. So, what we seem to have is a tennis player, probably lost in an early round, went to the beach, got a tan, and a tattoo, and then . . ."

"Met her demise," said Morgan. "I like the analysis, Salamander. Let's see where it leads." He turned to Grave. "You and Blunt take Salamander with you to the country club. Find out what you can about anyone who's lost and fits the description."

Grave nodded. "Sounds good."

"And let's split up the work on the tattoo parlors. How many of them are there, anyway?"

"There are fifteen in the Greater Crabopolis," said Snoot, "but I think we should focus on parlors along the beach or near the country club. That works the number down to, um, four."

"Okay," said Morgan. "You and Loblolly take two, and Charlize and Smithers-Watson will take the other two."

"Do we have a pic of the tattoo?" said Loblolly.

"Yes," said Salamander. "I snapped one at the scene." She pulled out her camera, a Leica MiniMight 50X, and pulled the pic up on the screen. "Here you go."

Loblolly gasped. "Oh, oh . . . that's *my* tattoo."

Snoot pushed her aside and looked at the image. "Holy crap, mine, too."

"In exactly the same place," said Loblolly.

"On the right thigh," said Snoot.

"High up," said Loblolly.

"Exactly," said Grave, then caught himself. "I guess."

Morgan rolled his eyes. He knew Grave and Loblolly were an item. "So, where did you get that tattoo, Loblolly?"

"We got it at Tiger Jimmy's on the Beach. A girl bonding kind of thing. A partner thing."

"All right, you two take Tiger Jimmy's and one other, and Charlize will take the rest."

"What about me?" said Detective Freeman.

"Well, God, I'm holding down the fort while you collect security footage from all the cameras at Skunk 'n Donuts and around the square." He turned back to the others. "Okay, get to it!"

7

The Crab Cove Country Club sprawled across two hundred acres of prime land hard upon the Chesapeake Bay. Its 18-hole golf course was second to none, and had hosted hundreds of professional events over the years. The Clubhouse and its surrounding swimming pools and tennis courts sat in the center of its beachfront, only a few steps from an immaculate white-sand beach, where the richest of the rich of Crab Cove boiled in the sun and sipped umbrella drinks from May through August.

Grave and Blunt pulled up at the front of the Clubhouse, followed shortly by Salamander on her hovercycle. As Grave and Blunt extricated themselves from the little car, Salamander dropped her cycle to the ground and ran to a practice green near the front door.

She dropped to her knees and ran her fingers across the grass. "What is this?"

Grave was the first to reach her. "What are you doing?"

She pointed at the close-cropped grass. "What is this?"

"Grass."

"No, it can't be. I've googled grass many times on Mars, and this is not grass."

"But it is," said Grave. "A special blend that grows tight and short, which makes it easier for the golf ball to move along its surface and into that hole over there."

"Truly?"

"Yes."

"It is a wonder. Like the felt top of my pool table back on Mars. But *alive*."

"What's going on," said Blunt, walking up.

"Putting green," said Grave.

Barry, Grave's personal drone, and Object, Blunt's drone, zoomed over their heads and hovered.

"What's up?" said Barry.

"Need help?" said Object.

"No, everything is okay," said Grave. "Salamander just had a moment with the grass."

Barry waggled in the air. "A moment?"

"Never mind, not important," said Grave. "Come on, everyone, let's find the manager of this place."

"Wait," said Salamander. "What's that sound?"

Grave listened intently. "Oh, that's the sound of tennis balls being hit with rackets. The tournament is on, remember?"

"Oh," said Salamander. "Can we see that, too? Oh, and the beach! I've never seen the ocean."

Grave felt like he was talking to an excited toddler. "Yes, if we have time, but now we have to talk to people, gather evidence, right?"

Salamander nodded. "Right, right." She ran her hands over the grass one last time, and stood. "Let's go."

They walked into the clubhouse and approached the concierge, a dour young woman in a black pantsuit who would have been better employed as an undertaker.

She got right to the point. "How might I help you?"

"Detective Grave, Crab Cove Police," he said, waving his badge in front of her nose. "We'd like to see your manager, as well as anyone in charge of the tennis tournament."

She smirked, which went well with black. "I'm afraid they are both busy at the moment. The clubhouse and the tournament make heavy demands on them."

Salamander stepped forward and grabbed the woman by her lapels. "We will see them *now*, get them *now*."

Grave pulled Salamander away. "What she means is that, whatever they're doing, wherever they are now, we need to see them here, now."

"Get them," screamed Salamander.

The woman blanched and ran away, disappearing through a door marked *employees only*.

Grave turned to Salamander. "You can't do that. We're here to investigate, not interrogate. You scared the poor woman half to death."

"Well, she already looks half dead," said Salamander. "And look, my technique worked."

Grave turned to see two men walking toward them, scowls on their faces, followed by the concierge, who seemed to be using them as a shield.

The taller of the two men stopped in front of them, hands on hips. "What's the meaning of this?"

Salamander lunged for him.

8

Tiger Jimmy's was an institution on the boardwalk. Anyone seeking a tattoo would head there first, hoping to get inked by one of Jimmy's five artists, in an open-concept parlor of more than 2,000 square feet. And the better your idea for your tat, the better your chances of attracting the attention of Tiger Jimmy himself. His area was in the back, shielded by a red velvet curtain. When TJ worked his magic, he didn't like to be watched.

Loblolly and Snoot pushed through its doors at noon, just as the parlor was beginning its day. A dozen eager customers, most in bathing suits, poured in with them, jockeying for the attention of their favorite artist.

Loblolly spotted the young man who had given them their crab tattoos two years ago, and although she couldn't remember his name, she saw that he recognized them.

He was tall and muscular, his biceps bulging against a black tee shirt that seemed to be two sizes too small for him. Loblolly remembered the muscles, but it was his nose she remembered most. It looked like someone had smashed his nose flat with a mallet, making his pale blue eyes seem to bug out.

"Hey, you two," he said, "where've you been? It's been what, four years?"

"No, two," said Loblolly, flashing her badge.

He took a step back and held up his hands. "Whoa, what's this? I've been good. Paying the alimony every month like clockwork."

Loblolly rolled her eyes. "We're not here for you, um . . ."

"Donald. Dapper Don. You don't remember, do you?"

"No, sorry. I remember your face, but not your name."

"And what's the last name, Donald?"

"Blake." He looked back and forth at them. "So, what's this all about?"

"Our tattoos," said Snoot. "Or rather the tattoo we got specifically."

"What, you want to get them touched up?"

"No, not that," said Loblolly. "We'd like to know if you or one of the other artists tattooed a young woman last night. You know, with that tattoo."

"And like ours," said Loblolly. "High on her right thigh."

Dapper Don nodded, thinking. "Let me see now, I did two of them last night, but not on the thigh. Women, though."

"No," said Loblolly, "it has to be high thigh."

"Well, it's our most popular tattoo—simple, cheap, not too big, and easy for us. Plus, it's the first tattoo they see when they come in the parlor." He pointed at a print of the tattoo hanging from a cable that crisscrossed the parlor. "There, see. I tell you, so many of these kids come in not knowing what they want. I mean, think about it. You're coming into my parlor to get a tattoo, an image that will stay with you for *life*, and you don't know what you want? It boggles the mind."

Loblolly shook her head. "Yeah, well, I didn't know what I wanted either, but that crab just leaped out at me."

He held up his hands. "Not judging, not judging." He looked around the parlor. "Gimme a minute, will you, and let me check with the others."

"Okay," said Loblolly.

They watched as he walked around the parlor, whispering to each of the artists. Things didn't look good. Every artist shook his or her head, so Loblolly and Snoot were not surprised by his findings.

"No one else did one on the thigh."

Snoot pointed in the direction of Tiger Jimmy's curtain. "What about Tiger Jimmy?"

Dapper Don laughed out loud, then covered his mouth. "Sorry, I didn't mean to laugh so hard. No, TJ doesn't do simple tattoos like that. Like asking Picasso to ink a happy face on you. Besides, he wasn't even here last night."

Loblolly frowned. "Well, then, I guess we'll have to look elsewhere."

Dapper Don raised a finger. "How about a tat while you're here?"

Loblolly laughed. "No, I'm good."

"Me, too," said Snoot.

"Well, if you change your minds, I'm here till midnight."

9

Charlize and Smithers walked into Yahoo Tattoo, a bell jangling above them, announcing their presence. The parlor was small, with a cash register on a small table at the front, along with a single chair for anyone who might be waiting for a tattoo. A black velvet curtain separated the register area from the tattoo station, where someone was now grunting.

An old man with a long, unruly white beard poked his head out from behind the curtain. "Tattoo?"

Charlize held up her badge. "No, just some information."

He stepped out from behind the curtain, revealing a short, rail-thin man dressed in an orange jumpsuit covered with military patches. His face was pink, and his shiny bulbous nose was red, like the nose of a heavy drinker. He squinted at her, his dark gray eyes leveling on her. "Information?"

"Yes, we're trying to identify where a young woman got a crab tattoo last night."

"A crab, huh?"

"Yes."

"Was she pretty?"

"Yes, very."

"Ah, and did she have blond hair?"

"Yes, she did."

"And would this have been late last night?"

"We think so, yes."

"And would the tattoo have been on her right upper thigh?"

Charlize beamed. "Yes, so she was here?"

He shrugged. "Maybe. Can you tell me more about the tattoo?"

Smithers stepped in front of Charlize, holding up an image of the tattoo. "Here, this is the tattoo."

The old man frowned, then shook his head. "Not my tattoo. This one is from a book. I do all of mine freehand."

Charlize and Smithers slumped simultaneously, Charlize imagining sails without wind, Smithers imagining a slowly deflating balloon, but without the little squeak and whoopee cushion sound at the end.

"Why so glum?" he said.

"She wasn't here," said Charlize.

The man laughed, which was more of a failed cackle. "Oh, she was here, all right. Just insisted I do the tattoo from the book. Not that I would. Not that I ever would. So I just gave her a copy of the Chamber of Commerce brochure listing all the parlors in the Greater Crabopolis."

"Did you recommend a specific parlor?" said Smithers.

He shook his head.

"Did you see which direction she went when she left?"

"No. I gave her the brochure. She sat right there in that chair, and started reading. After a while, I went in back to my chair in the back. I heard the bell when she left, of course, but I didn't bother to look."

"What about her personal drone?"

He shrugged. "She didn't have one as far as I could see. Could have been outside, of course. Dunno."

Charlize nodded. They weren't going to get anything more from this guy. She handed him a card. "If you think of anything else, anything she said or did, please get in touch."

He nodded. "I can tell you one thing right now."

"Oh?" said Smithers.

"Yeah, she seemed nervous. Kept glancing at the door, like she was expecting someone."

"Got it," said Smithers. "So if you think of anything more . . ."

"I'll give you guys a call. So, is that it?"

"Yep," said Smithers.

"Good, now I can get back to my book."

"What are you reading?" said Charlize.

"That new bestseller, *No Expectations*, from Charles Dickens."

"Oh, another of those AI books."

"Yeah, and it's really good."

"Glad to hear it." She gave him a nod and walked to the door, but Charlize didn't move. "Charlize, you coming?"

She held up a finger. "One thing more, sir."

"Yes?"

"Can you spare another of those brochures with the business locator map?"

"Sure thing." He went behind the register and pulled a brochure out of a cardboard box. "I've got a ton of them, so here."

Charlize took the brochure and opened it to the map. "Have a look, Smithers."

Smithers moved beside her and looked down at the map. "What?"

"If you were her, where would you go?"

"I don't know."

"Think about it, Smithers. You want a tattoo and you're nervous, maybe being followed. Where would you go?"

"Um, to the nearest one?"

Charlize smiled. "Exactly."

10

Grave caught Salamander in mid-lunge and tugged her back behind him. "Let me do the talking," he whispered before turning back to the two men.

He showed his badge. "I'm Detective Grave, and this is Sergeant Blunt and Detective Salamander.

"I'm Manley Morris, club director, and this is Jacky Pompo, tournament executive. And now perhaps you can tell me why your detective manhandled my concierge."

The two men could not have been more different. Morris was tall and thin, and dressed in a dark blue three-piece suit. He was ghostly pale with a thin black moustache twisted at each end in a way that suggested Salvador Dali. Pompo, on the other hand, was thick as a bull, dressed in tennis whites, his arms and legs tanned and lush with blond hair. An old pro, now turned to management but still clinging to the look.

Salamander started to move again, but Grave held her back. "My apologies for that. A young woman has been murdered and we are trying to move as quickly as possible to identify her and her assailant. Your concierge was slowing us down, and my detective was trying to speed things up. A tad too harshly, of course."

Morris shook his head. "Whatever. So what's this about a murder?"

"A young woman, found in the town square. From her build, particularly the difference between her right arm and her left, we think she was a tennis player, perhaps one competing here."

"My goodness," said Morris. "Can you describe her?"

"Young, maybe seventeen or eighteen, blonde, shapely, very strong right arm, particularly the forearm."

Pompo bent over at the waist and shook his head. "No, no, no."

"What?" said Grave.

Pompo took a deep breath. "One of our players didn't show for her quarter-finals match this morning. Heather Van Hinkle."

"Oh, my god," said Morris. "I talked to her just yesterday."

"What time?" said Grave.

He looked at the ceiling, searching for the answer. "About two or so. She was dressed for the beach. Red bikini topped with a sheer blue coat-like thing for modesty, a large beige purse over her shoulder, and beach clogs, also red. Oh, and her toes were painted a pale blue. Does that help?"

Grave shrugged. "I don't know." He turned to Blunt. "Did you notice her toenails?"

"Yes," said Blunt. "They were a pale blue."

"Then in all probability, it was her, your Ms. Heather Van Hinkle. She was found early this morning in front of the Skunk 'n Donuts. Completely naked. No sign of any clothing."

"Jesus," said Pompo. "Who would do such a thing?"

"She was absolutely loved, detective. A darling girl, a real up-and-comer."

Grave nodded. "Can you think of any reason someone might want to kill her?"

They both shook their heads vigorously, as if the question was absurd.

"Is her family here?"

"Her father," said Pompo. "Koos Van Hinkle."

"What about her coach?"

"Larry Flan? Yes, of course."

"We'd like to speak to them, the father first, and then the coach and, if you can arrange it, as many of the other players as possible."

"Of course, of course," said Morris.

"But not the players who have matches today," said Pompo. "I don't want to upset them."

"That makes sense," said Grave. "But all the others, please."

"Very well," said Morris. He turned to the concierge. "Our concierge here, Sally Fifth, will make the arrangements. Sally, set them up in Conference Room Six. Refreshments and so on."

Her frown grew deeper with every word.

"Thank you," said Grave. He turned to Fifth. "If you could show us to the room . . ."

She nodded. "This way."

"A second," he said.

He pulled Blunt aside. "Have Object spread the word that we have identified the victim, and see if Captain Morgan can delay our meeting until four so we can do as many interviews as possible."

"Right," said Blunt, turning for the door.

Grave motioned Salamander closer. "And as for you, you and I will have to have a talk about your behavior. You can't just grab a person like that."

"She was being disrespectful."

Grave rolled his eyes. "We'll discuss this later. For now, let's focus on finding the murderer."

She shrugged. "Whatever."

11

Sparky received the message from Blunt first and outraced Midnight to Loblolly and Snoot, who were about to go into RoboTattoo, one of those new parlors where the tattoos were applied robotically. Even the largest and most intricate tattoos could be applied perfectly in less than ten minutes.

"Heather Van Hinkle, eh?" said Loblolly. "Never heard of her."

"Really?" said Snoot. "She's amazing. Was amazing. A terrific backhand and a deceptively fast serve. They called her serve 'the ghost,' it was so hard to see."

"A damn shame."

"Yeah." She nodded at the tattoo parlor. "Let's do this."

"Right."

A simdroid resembling Johnny Depp dressed as Captain Jack Sparrow greeted them as soon as they entered the parlor, sweeping off his tri-corner hat and executing a deep bow that would have made the real Johnny Depp proud. "Welcome to RoboTattoo, where you don't need to be a pirate to steal a tattoo good as gold."

"Actually, we're only here for information, not a tattoo," said Loblolly.

"We're trying to determine whether a young tennis player, Heather Van Hinkle, received a crab tattoo in your parlor yesterday," said Snoot.

Captain Sparrow seemed crestfallen. "No tattoo?"

Loblolly and Snoot shook their heads.

"Pity. We have the finest machines, the best of inks, and the lowest of prices. What if I make you a deal? A tattoo for each of you at half the price? How about that?"

"Nope," said Snoot.

"And a nope from me as well," said Loblolly. "So, do you know whether Ms. Van Hinkle was here yesterday?"

Captain Sparrow put his hat back on and motioned them to a small console near the suite of robotic tattoo equipment. "If she did, we'd have a record of her visit here." He started typing on the keyboard, then stopped. "Did you say Hinkle or Winkle?"

"Hinkle with an H," said Loblolly. "Van. Van Hinkle."

"Right," said Sparrow. He spoke as he typed. "Heather Van Hinkle, not Winkle." He hit enter and a small clock appeared, its hands moving to indicate that the machine was considering the question. And then the clock's hands stopped, the clock disappeared, and an error message appeared.

ERROR 16B: NO SUCH CUSTOMER

"Sorry," said Sparrow

"Wait a second," said Snoot. "Maybe she didn't use her real name."

"Oh, a clever vixen, then."

"Maybe," said Loblolly. "Key in crab tattoo."

"Excellent idea," said Sparrow. He turned back to the keyboard and entered *crab tattoo*. The clock appeared, the hands spun, and a new message appeared.

JASON WORTH, CRAB TATTOO 27
DOLLY DANGER, CRAB TATTOO 12
BITSY CUSTARD, CRAB TATTOO 15
ETHEL MELLON, CRAB TATTOO 14

"Three possibilities," said Sparrow.

Snoot frowned. "Um, can you show us what those tattoos look like?"

"Yes, of course." He highlighted each tattoo, bringing up an image of each on the screen.

Loblolly shook her head. "No, no, no, and no."

"Not her tattoo," said Snoot. "Sorry to trouble you."

"Trouble? No, no, no, lovely ladies. It was my pleasure to be of assistance in your time of need. So, am I still unable to persuade you to partake of our vast selection of tattoos?"

"I'm afraid so," said Loblolly. "But we thank you for your efforts and your time."

Sparrow lifted Loblolly's hand and kissed it. "Please come again."

Then he turned and did the same with Snoot, who couldn't suppress a giggle.

12

Papa Joe's Tattoo and Piercing was the closest parlor, but neither Charlize nor Smithers could believe that anyone would think about going in, even given that it was located on the boardwalk. The windows to the little shop were encrusted with salt and dirt to the extent that only a few letters in the shop's name could be seen. An eerily glowing OPEN sign in the window could barely be seen.

"Do we go in?" said Smithers.

Charlize started to answer, but the door to the little shop swung open and a bald man no taller than Polk popped his bald head out. Unlike Polk, he was as round as a bowling ball, and had a white handlebar moustache that waved in the strong breeze coming off the Bay. He was dressed in beige shorts and a red tee shirt that exposed his hairy bellybutton. "Are you coming in, or what?"

Charlize nodded. "Yes, of course."

"Well, then, get in here."

Charlize and Smithers followed him in to the dimly lit shop. If anything, it was dirtier inside than out. Dust covered the countertops and shelves. Spider webs festooned the corners and the space between the blades of an old, nonfunctional ceiling fan. It seemed like a fitting place for a germ amusement park. "I'm Charlize Holmes and this is my partner, Doctor Smithers-Watson."

He extended a dirty hand. "I'm Papa Joe, artiste par excellence and the cheapest on the boardwalk. But you're not here for that, are you? Simdroids, right? Pretending to be Sherlock Holmes and his trusty doctor friend, Doctor Watson, am I right?"

"Yes," said Charlize. "Very perceptive. We're actually detectives with the Crab Cove Police Department, investigating a murder."

His eyes went wide. "A murder? You don't say. But why are you here, then?"

"We have reason to believe the victim, Heather Van Hinkle, came to your shop last night and got a small crab tattoo, and—"

"On her upper right thigh, yes. Oh my god, I can't believe it. She was so pretty, so sweet, and a good tipper."

Charlize smiled at Smithers. "We were right."

"So it seems," said Smithers.

Charlize turned back to the man. "We'd like details, please."

"Anything," he said. "I'm an open book."

"What time did she arrive?"

"Um, about eight or so, give or take. Dressed in a bikini and a little coat-like thing to cover herself a bit."

"How did she select that tattoo?"

"She had a little picture of it with her. She wanted that tattoo and that tattoo only. She said it was to match another person's tattoo."

"Did she say whose?"

"No, but she got a kind of dreamy look when she said it. So I figure it was a boyfriend or maybe even a girlfriend."

"Did she seem nervous?"

"A little, but that's common with a person's first tattoo. They really don't know what to expect."

"And how long did it take to give her the tattoo."

"It was a simple tattoo, so just fifteen minutes. Pity, I could have looked at those legs of hers for hours."

Charlize ignored the comment. "So she was out of here at about 8:15."

"Thereabouts, yes."

"Did she say where she was going?"

"Not exactly, but she did say she couldn't wait to show her friend the tattoo. It would be a surprise, she said."

"I see. Did you notice which way she went when she left?"

"To the right, actually. Down the boardwalk."

Charlize nodded. "Thank you for your help." She handed him a card. "If you think of anything else—"

"Wait," said Smithers. "Did she have a personal drone with her?"

Papa Joe frowned. "I'm not sure. When she left, I stood outside a while and watched her walk down the boardwalk. Couldn't help myself. She was that beautiful."

"But the drone?"

"One was trailing her, yes, about ten yards or so behind her, but it could have been someone else's."

"Can you describe it?" said Charlize.

"The body was bright orange, but the struts and blades were black."

Charlize turned to Smithers. "Anything else?"

He shook his head.

"Okay, then," said Charlize, extending her hand to Papa Joe. "Thanks again."

She made a mental note to disinfect her entire body at the earliest possible moment.

13

The small conference room provided by Sally Fifth was adequate. There was a long table with enough chairs on either side to conduct the interviews, but little else in the way of comfort. Still, Fifth had balanced the plain room with an ornate urn of coffee and a silver tray containing gourmet donuts from Squares on the Square, a bakery that offered a cinnamon-to-nuts line of square donuts with square holes. The holes themselves, called *cubettes*, were available in every flavor.

Grave had wolfed down two chocolate donuts and a handful of cinnamon cubettes before he even sat down. Salamander was skeptical, placing a single plain cubette into her mouth and then quickly spitting it out on her hand. "Too sweet."

Blunt had taken a pass, patting his stomach and shaking his head. "Diet."

Heather Van Hinkle's father, Koos, was the first to be led into the room, and Grave could tell by his posture and the deep sadness in his eyes that he already knew the worst. He was wearing all-white tennis togs, revealing deeply tanned skin, with a bright yellow sweater draped over his shoulders and tied around his neck. There was no doubt that he played tennis, a lot. His left forearm was huge. His hair was buzz cut on the sides but long on the top, with traces of gray in his otherwise mouse brown hair. Judging from the wrinkles on his forehead and the crow's feet around his blue eyes, he looked to be a man in his late forties.

"They told me," he said, sitting down opposite Grave. "I should have called the police sooner. She was due at a cocktail party at eight, but didn't show. Not like her. Not like her at all. She was always on time. Being late was unthinkable. In fact, she always showed up for her matches early, sometimes even before the crowd arrived. I thought that perhaps she just wanted some alone time before her quarter final match." He sighed and took a deep breath. "What can you tell me, detective?"

"First," said Grave, "please accept our sincere condolences for your loss. We know this is a hard time for you, so if you'd rather talk to us at a later time, we can do that."

Van Hinkle waved him off. "No, I want to be as helpful to you as I can, so we can catch the bastard."

Grave nodded. "Very well. I'm Detective Simon Grave and this is Sergeant Blunt and Detective Salamander. We'll be interviewing everyone she came in contact with during her stay here. Her coach, fellow players—anyone and everyone. While we are doing this, other teams of detectives are currently searching Crab Cove to find out where she received a tattoo last night."

Van Hinkle screwed up his face. "Tattoo? Why in hell would she get a tattoo? She was very proud of her body and her skin. She would never get a tattoo in a million years."

"But she did," said Salamander. "A crab. Small. Black. On her thigh."

"Oh, my god," said Van Hinkle. "Why on Earth?"

"So," said Grave, "the medical examiner has her now and will provide an update later this afternoon. For now, all we know is that her body was found in front of a donut shop in the town square. Estimated time of death was two this morning, so one of the things we'll be working on is creating a timeline of her whereabouts since yesterday afternoon."

"Good," said Van Hinkle. "That sounds right. So when can I see my daughter?"

"After a few questions, if you don't mind." He turned to Blunt. "Get in touch with Polk and set something up as soon as possible."

"Right," said Blunt, pushing back his chair. "Be back in a few minutes." He pushed his chair back in and left the room.

"Thank you, detective," said Van Hinkle. "Now, what can I tell you?"

"Do you know anyone who would do her harm?"

Van Hinkle shook his head. "Not a single person."

"What about fellow players? Any grudges."

"Not that I'm aware of. Yes, things are heated during matches, but any animosity is left on the court."

"So she never complained to you about anyone?"

"No, never."

"What about her coach, Larry Flan?"

Van Hinkle rolled his eyes. "He was always hard on her, too hard on her at times, but it was tough love. No, it couldn't be him."

Grave turned to Salamander. "Any additional questions at this point?"

Salamander looked surprised that she had been asked to participate. "Um, yes, as a matter of fact." She turned to Van Hinkle.

"Getting a tattoo can be an act of love or an act of defiance or rebellion, among other reasons. Did your daughter have a love interest?"

"No, absolutely not."

"Oh, what makes you so sure?"

"Her schedule. The training, the matches, the travel—there isn't a second in between."

"Not even with other tennis players?"

Van Hinkle shook his head. "I've seen nothing to indicate that. I can only conclude that she did something or went somewhere yesterday that got her killed. Lovers? No, that's impossible, too."

"What about defiance, then."

Van Hinkle rolled his eyes. "Detective, please, until yesterday, she was the happiest young lady in the world."

Salamander nodded. "Of course she was. Okay, one last question for now, at least from me. When was the last time you saw her?"

"Lunch, around twelve-thirty or so. She seemed fine. In fact, she said she was going to spend some time at the pool."

Salamander turned to Grave. "Sir, any more questions?"

Grave shook his head. "Not at this time, but we'll be getting back to you, I'm sure." He pushed his card across the table to Van Hinkle. "We'll be here until about three, so feel free to interrupt our interviews if you think of something. After that, give me a call, any time, day or night."

"Thank you," said Van Hinkle. "I'll do that."

They watched him leave the room and close the door behind him.

"So," Grave said, "what do you think?"

"About him?"

"Yes."

"All right. Left-handed. No wedding ring. Not even a tan line that would suggest a ring. Hair plugs, contacts, that ridiculous yellow sweater, so I'd say he's pretty vain. Haircut inappropriate for his age. Kept glancing at me. I think he likes them young. And most important of all, a follow-up question: did he really file a missing person's report? And if so, when?"

Grave blinked. "We can verify that one way or the other when we get back to the station. Anything else?"

"I don't think he gives a hoot about his daughter."

Grave started to reply, but the door swung open and Blunt walked back in.

"Did you talk with Polk?" said Grave.

"Yeah, but I didn't get a chance to ask about Van Hinkle identifying his daughter."

"What? Why?"

"Let me guess," said Salamander. "Another body."

Blunt's eyes went wide. "Yes."

"With a crab tattoo."

And wider still. "Yes."

14

The body had been hidden under a flattened cardboard box under the boardwalk, in a less frequented part of the beach where the homeless made their makeshift camps of boxes and bags. Officer Larrys had cordoned off the area, much to the dismay and anger of its residents, who were also being held for questioning.

Grave, Blunt, and Salamander were the last to arrive, pushing their way through a score of bystanders and under the crime scene tape.

"What have we got, captain?" said Grave.

Morgan turned and nodded at him. "A body, of course. Another young woman, about the same age as Van Hinkle."

Polk, who was kneeling next to the body, looked up at them. Pretty, brunette, naked, and believe it or not, the same damn tattoo."

"On the thigh?" said Salamander.

"No, on her left shoulder." He pointed to the victim's arm.

Salamander cocked her head. "Ah, that's a surprise, but interesting nonetheless."

"Do we have a time of death?" said Grave.

"Not precisely, but I think I'll find it matches the other woman within minutes."

"And do you have a time of death for her?"

"Yes, the Van Hinkle woman died at about 1:45, give or take a few minutes."

Salamander went to her knees to get a closer look at the body. "The tattoo is old and faded. Her arms are toned, but thin. No sign of the muscular imbalance that comes with playing tennis. But the tattoos connect them in some way. We just have to figure that out."

"Exactly," said Morgan. He looked at his watch. "So here's what we're going to do. Polk, take the body to the morgue, but then join us at the station at 4:30, so we can all review what we've found and what we know about the Van Hinkle case."

"Fine," said Polk.

Morgan turned to the others. "Now let's learn as much as we can about the scene. Grave, I'd like you, Blunt, and Salamander to split up and interview those people over there. See if they saw anything."

"Right," said Grave.

Morgan turned to Charlize. "I'd like you and Smithers to do a quick survey of the scene. Are her clothes here somewhere? Are Van Hinkle's? And so on."

He turned to Detective Freeman. "And you, God, take a look at the security cameras around this stretch of beach and boardwalk, including businesses."

"That will take several hours."

"Collect what you can before the meeting, and then come back."

"Right."

Morgan turned to Loblolly and Snoot. "And I'd like you guys to talk to the shopkeepers above us who might have been open that late. Perhaps they saw something."

He looked at them all. "Okay, folks, do what you can between now and 4:15, then meet me back at the station. Are we clear?"

Everyone nodded.

"Okay, get to it."

15

Medical Examiner Jeremy Polk was the last to arrive, pushing into the conference room carrying a stack of photographs of the two young women.

"About time," said Morgan.

Polk smirked. "Which I have little of, so can we get this show on the road?"

"Of course," said Morgan, sitting down with the others. "You have the floor."

Polk sat the photographs down at the head of the conference table, one stack for each girl. "These are pics of the girls. Pass them around."

Loblolly picked up one stack, took a photograph, and passed the stack to Snoot. Grave picked up the other stack, took a photo, and passed the stack on to God.

"Okay," said Polk, looking down at a document containing his findings. "Let's start with Ms. Van Hinkle. Time of death: 1:45 a.m. plus or minus. Manner of death: poison. She died instantly, meaning she died in front of Skunk 'n Donuts."

Grave raised his hand. "Wait a minute, she was naked. No sign of her clothes or her drone."

"Exactly," said Polk. "As hard as it is to believe, she may have been running naked through downtown Crab Cove until she met her fate at the donut shop." He turned to the rest of the detectives. "Now, if you please, let me finish."

He waited until he had seen everyone nod. "The bottoms of her feet were cut up, reinforcing the idea of flight. So one of the questions to answer would be, *flight from what?*"

Salamander raised her hand. "I agree with the question, but there's a flaw in your basic argument."

"Oh?"

"The fact that the poison works instantly and the fact that her feet were bloody does not necessarily mean she was killed in front of the donut shop. She could have run some distance, been apprehended by the murderer, killed, and then dropped in front of Skunk 'n Donuts."

"Um," said Polk.

"She's right," said Grave.

Polk nodded. "Very well, another question, then. Where exactly was she killed?"

"Go on," said Morgan.

Polk looked back down at the document. "Oh, otherwise, her body was unharmed. No signs of a struggle, no defensive wounds, no signs of penetration. Nothing."

He turned to Morgan. "Should I go on to Victim Number Two, or do you guys want to discuss this?"

Morgan ran a hand across his bald head. "I think we should discuss this a little before you move on. From my perspective, the key will be what we find on the CCTV cameras around the square." He turned to God. "How is that going?"

God, aka Detective Morgan Freeman, held up a piece of paper. "There are now eighteen cameras on the square, including two that cover Skunk 'n Donuts. I've collected the tapes, but haven't had a chance to review them."

"What about the tapes from the boardwalk?" said Salamander.

"You mean for the second victim?"

"For her, yes, but also for Van Hinkle."

"Right," said Charlize. "We know Van Hinkle got her tattoo on the boardwalk, at Papa Joe's, around eight or so."

"And Papa Joe's is located directly above where we found the second body," said Smithers, "on the boardwalk."

"So," said Salamander, "I was thinking we could trace her movements from the tattoo parlor to the square, using the CCTV footage."

"Yes, of course," said God, "but I haven't collected all that footage yet. There wasn't time before this meeting."

"All right," said Morgan. "You'll have to get back to that after this meeting."

"Right," said God, "but I did assign three Officer Larrys to collect the tapes in my absence. We might even have the tapes before we wrap up today."

"Great," said Morgan. "All right, so the next step on the Van Hinkle case is to review that footage. If she was killed at Skunk 'n Donuts, the killer should be there, too." He turned to Polk. "Are you sure she would have died instantly?"

Polk nodded. "Oh, yeah. Within two seconds."

Morgan smiled. "So we definitely should have him on tape."

Salamander raised her hand. "Unless the poison was delivered from a distance."

Morgan turned to Polk. "Is that possible?"

Polk shook his head. "I don't see how that's possible. The poison was delivered by needle injection, but there's no sign of the needle."

Salamander held up her hand again. "We had a case on Mars where the needle itself vaporized after the strike."

"Wow," said Polk. "I've never heard of that before."

"If I'm right, her body, particularly around the injection site, will have a fine residue of an organic polymer. I forget the name of it, but the marker you'd be looking for is trace elements of zinc and tin."

Polk nodded. "I'll get right on that."

"Good," said Morgan, "but let's hope the poison was delivered close up."

Blunt raised a hand. "There's one other possibility, sir."

"Oh?"

"Yes, as we've learned before, the murderer could have been invisible."

Morgan rolled his eyes and groaned.

16

Polk moved on to the second victim. "There's not too much I can tell you at this point. Same tattoo as Van Hinkle, but larger and on the left upper arm at the shoulder. Could mean they know each other, but it's also the most popular tattoo among tourists, so perhaps it's just a coincidence. Okay, time of death was 1:30 a.m., pretty close to Van Hinkle's time of death and preceding it. Manner of death—exactly the same as Van Hinkle's, poison by lethal injection. No sign of struggle, no defensive wounds. Same wounds on the feet, from running barefoot." He paused. "If I had to guess, I'd say we're talking about the same attacker and that both victims knew their attacker, or at least the attacks were a surprise, giving them no time to defend themselves."

He looked over at Salamander, wondering whether she would interrupt again, but she just sat there, shaking her head.

"So that's it for me," he said.

"Thanks, Jeremy. Head on back to the morgue and check out Salamander's disappearing needle theory."

"Right, right," said Polk. He gave everyone a quick wave and then left the room.

Morgan waited until the door closed. "So, what do we know so far from the crime scene? Charlize, what have you got?"

"We did a preliminary search of the scene, but found nothing that could be called a clue. There was clothing all over the place, but we don't know whether it belongs to the victim or the under-boardwalk residents. We bagged each item—there were about twenty—and sent them to the morgue to see if we can get a DNA match with the victim or victims. Also, because our search time was brief, we kept the crime scene in place, so we can search further, if necessary."

"Good," said Morgan, turning to Loblolly. "So did any of the boardwalk residents see anything?"

She shook her head. "I think they know something, but they're not saying."

"They don't want to be snitches," said Snoot. "It's their code."

Grave raised a hand. "By any chance was Crab Cake Johnny among them? I know he beds down there sometimes."

"Who's Crab Cake Johnny?" said Salamander.

"A homeless trash picker, philosopher, and trusted informant. If anyone at the scene saw something or did something, he'll be able to find out." He turned to Morgan. "I can follow up on that, captain."

"Okay," said Morgan. "It's getting late in the day, but if you could follow up with him on your way home, that would be great."

"Sure, no problem."

"So," said Morgan, "any feedback from the shopkeepers?"

Loblolly shook her head. "We were able to talk with fifteen shopkeepers along the boardwalk, so we still have another thirty to go. The ones we did talk to saw nothing."

"What about Papa Joe's?"

"No, Papa Joe's was closed and dark."

"In the middle of the day?"

"There was a sign in the window," said Snoot. "Closed due to illness."

"Odd," said Charlize. "He was a dirty man, but seemed healthy enough when we talked to him."

Morgan nodded. "It is strange. Charlize, see what you can do about finding him and bringing him in for questioning. He may be our man, and he may be on the run."

17

She really was a stranger in a strange land. Grave watched her as she gobbled down a double order of cheesy fries from Dolores on the Beach, Crab Cove's go-to site for french-fries. She was like a small child, experiencing a wonder for the first time. All her rough edges and her no-nonsense demeanor disappeared. He fully expected her to start giggling at any minute.

She caught him looking. "What?"

"You."

She put two more fries in her mouth. "Me, what about me?"

"How much you're enjoying those fries."

"First time."

"I can see that, and I'm glad you're enjoying them."

She rolled her eyes. "Just try living in a cave on Mars, where everything you eat is hydroponic or comes out of a squeeze tube." She held up the cup of fries. "These, these are a marvel in a world of marvels."

"Even better than the frozen custard?"

The giggle finally burst from her. She held a hand to her head. "What did you call it, that feeling?"

"A brain freeze. You ate it too fast."

"Ooh, lesson learned, and yes, I enjoyed the fries more than the custard. My tastes tend toward salty. So, what's next? Everywhere I look, there's something new to see, to taste, to explore, and I want it all."

Grave took a sip of his coffee and smiled at her. He could have jumped to the right answer, that they had to get back to business and find Crab Cake Johnny, but he opted to turn the question back on her. "I don't know. What would you like to do next?"

"Sex, I want to have sex."

The spray of coffee that burst from his mouth glistened in the late afternoon sun.

18

God ran his hand over her and smiled. "Is this sexy, or what?"

"What?" said Captain Morgan.

"Her," said God. "The new equipment."

"It's new?"

"The CCTV-5000 Syncolator XL? Yes, absolutely."

"How is it better?"

"In just about every way. It's smaller, faster, more powerful, and it can do things automatically instead of manually."

"Okay, let's get started."

God nodded and pushed the start button. The lights in the room automatically went dark and a bright, crisp image of Heather Van Hinkle's body came up on the far wall.

"Here we go," said God. "She's already dead at this point. Just lying there in front of the Skunk 'n Donuts. Now watch."

He turned a nob and the body jumped up and started running backwards down the sidewalk.

"She's wearing clothes," said Morgan, "but I didn't see her losing her clothes. What the hell is going on?"

"Not sure, but do you see what the machine is doing?"

"Running in reverse?"

"Yes, but more. The Syncolator has already synced and used the images from three separate cameras. It's synched them automatically and seamlessly. It anticipates when the target is about to move out of range of one camera and then auto-syncs it to the other cameras about to come in range."

Morgan was suitably impressed. "Wow. So how far back can we take her?"

"Three blocks, all the way to the boardwalk. Once we have the downloads from the other cameras, we'll be able to trace her all the way back to where she lost her shoes."

"Good." Morgan pointed at the Syncolator. "Make it go forward now, so we can see her final moments. And take it slow. Let's see when that dart or whatever the hell it was hits her."

God hit another button and Heather Van Hinkle ran slowly to her death.

"Stop," said Morgan, and God complied. "Back it up just a tad. Did you see it, a kind of flash?"

"No, I didn't," said God, "but I'll back it up."

"Very slowly now," said Morgan.

She was running, occasionally looking over her shoulder, and then her head seemed to slam to the right. As it did, there was a flash of some kind, the whole image becoming brighter but fuzzier, as if a bright cloud had passed by in an instant.

"Wow," said God.

"Indeed," said Morgan.

"What the hell was that?"

"I don't know. Roll it back and let's take another look."

They did, again and again, but they learned nothing more.

"Give me an hour or so," said God. "I'll adjust the Syncolator so we can slow it down further, maybe find out what that flash was all about."

Morgan slumped back in his chair. "All right, I'll leave it to you. Come get me when you're ready."

God said nothing. He was already removing the side panel of the Syncolator, looking for the fine adjustment screws.

19

Salamander laughed, perhaps too hard for the stunned Grave. "Not you, old man, so take that look off your face. Sex with you? Oh my dear god." She screwed up her face like she had just tasted something bad, like a Martian hydroponic Brussel sprout.

Whatever look his face had taken while he faced Salamander, he tried to change it quickly. He always thought that an embarrassed chuckle was appropriate in these situations, so he gave a chuckle a try as he shook his head, waved a negative hand, and backed away from her. "Oh, no, no, no. That would be silly. I was just surprised that sex got so high up on your list so quickly." He pointed at the Bay. "You haven't even dipped your toes in the Chesapeake."

She looked at the Bay, and nodded. "Yes, you're right. It's just that there's nothing like a long space voyage to spark the fantasies of a Martian virgin."

He didn't know what to say to that, so he pointed at her French-fries, which numbered just two. "More fries?"

She smiled. "You need to work on your segues, Grave. No, let's go find this Crab Cake Johnny of yours."

"Right, right. Let's head down the boardwalk. We'll probably find him standing by a trashcan. He loves day-old fries and cheeseburgers."

"Sounds charming."

"More like fragrant. We'll probably smell him long before we see him."

"Oh, wonderful."

They walked down the boardwalk, passing surfer shops and souvenir shops (tee-shirt: "I got crabs in Crab Cove") and shops that specialized in high-priced, low-quality "discount" clothing and flip-flops. Finally, after passing six trashcans without success, a light breeze brought a heavy odor.

Grave sniffed. "It's him. We're getting close."

Salamander felt like she was going to retch. "Oh, my god, what is that?"

"I've tried to come up with a description of it over the years, but the only way to explain it is, that can only be Crab Cake Johnny." He pointed down the boardwalk where a man was hovered over a trashcan. "There, that's him."

Crab Cake Johnny was a spectacle on legs. He was old and thin and bent over, with clothing that came straight from the Mars Surplus shop down the boardwalk: an old Mars mining helmet, complete with cut-off oxygen hoses; silvery Mylar trousers, the kind worn by early astronauts; a biker's vest, complete with a large Sons of Irony patch on the back; and footwear that included a scuffed brown sandal on one foot and a Martian miner's boot on the other, which probably explained his limp.

He had long white hair and a matching beard that came all the way to his waist. His mouth was forever screwed up into a sour expression and his pale blue eyes seemed frozen into a perpetual squint, like he couldn't believe or understand what he was seeing.

Salamander took all this in before stepping up to him and cold-cocking him, the man dropping to the ground like the proverbial sack of Martian ore.

"God dammit, dad. God dammit!"

20

Papa Joe's illness sign was still in the window when Charlize and Smithers returned. She rapped on the front door, to no effect. She rapped louder, again to no effect. She turned to Smithers. "Can you see anything?"

"Not a thing. All is dark."

She tried the doorknob. Locked. She took a few steps back so she could see the second-floor windows. The shades were drawn and there was no sign of light around the edges. "What do you think?"

"Gone, I guess, or just ignoring us."

"Tell you what. Give Drone Central a call and see if we can get a number for him."

"But there was no drone around the last time we were here."

"Even so." She looked up and down the boardwalk. "While you do that, I'll check out the backdoor. Some of these shopkeepers sleep at the rear of their stores."

"All right," said Smithers. "Be careful."

The alleyway out back was paved with crushed oyster shells, so there was no way Charlize could sneak up on the backdoor.

And once she got there, there seemed to be no need. The door was locked and the shades were drawn, and no amount of pounding stirred anyone inside. Of interest, however, was the lack of a vehicle in the owner's space.

She walked, or rather crunched, her way back to the front of the store.

"Any luck?" said Smithers.

"No, everything's locked tight. How about you?"

"The man has no drone. How is it possible for a human to not have a drone?"

Charlize shrugged. "Papa Joe didn't look like a man of this century. Maybe he's using a cellphone."

"A cellphone? They're illegal."

"Hey, we're talking about Papa Joe."

Smithers nodded. "Maybe we can get a home address for him down at the boardwalk office."

"Good idea," said Charlize. "And let's give God a call. Maybe the CCTV footage will show him leaving."

"Or not," said Smithers.

"If so, we'll get a warrant and gain entry."

"Sounds good," said Smithers. He pointed down the boardwalk. "The office is this way, about ten stores down."

21

Captain Henry Morgan, no stranger to confusion, looked at the screen once, then again, and finally a third time before allowing that confusion to take over. "I just don't understand this."

"Nor do I," said God, "but it is what it is."

What it was, to use a technical term, was a barely detectible *flash* lasting no more than a few milliseconds. And during that brief moment, *something* appeared and disappeared. No more than a shadow that flickered and was gone.

"A flash?" said Morgan.

"Yes," said God.

"Can you get better definition?"

"No."

"So we're stuck with a shadow of something lasting, what, two milliseconds?"

"Two point six to be exact."

"What could it be?"

"I don't know but it seems to be directly related to the death of Ms. Van Hinkle. After that flash, she's no longer clothed and just drops to the ground like the proverbial sack of oysters."

"We may need to get some scientific advice on this one, but first I'd like everyone else to take a look at this flash. Get in touch with everyone and tell them I'm moving the morning meeting up to 7:00 a.m."

"Right," said God. "Will do."

22

Grave and Salamander sat in a corner of the waiting room, waiting for a nurse to escort them to the bedside of Crab Cake Johnny, who had been admitted for observation.

"How's your hand?" said Grave.

Salamander held up her bandaged hand. "Sore."

"You're lucky you didn't break it."

She shrugged. "He has a soft face."

"You realize he could file a complaint against you."

She laughed. "As if. No, I know my bastard father. He'll just slither back to the boardwalk."

"Well, I could write you up as well. Probably should."

She gave him a look. "Really?"

"Maybe. Why did you do it?"

She let out a big sigh. "It was a long story not too many years ago, but I've managed to whittle it down to less than twenty words over the last few years. He abused my mom. I stuck him in the head with a dinner fork. And he left."

Grave began counting on his fingers. "So that's, um, what?"

"Seventeen, and now I can add three more: *knocked him out*."

A nurse appeared through double doors on the far side of the waiting room and called out, "Grave?"

"That's us," said Grave, pulling Salamander up from her chair. "Come on."

They followed the nurse back through the double doors and down a long white hallway that smelled of disinfectant and loneliness.

"How is he?" said Grave.

The nurse said nothing, leading them into a hospital room with two beds, one occupied by Crab Cake Johnny, who seemed none too pleased to see them, and another man, who seemed to share the same sentiment.

Grave nodded at the other man. "I'm Detective Grave and this is my colleague, Detective Salamander."

The man looked them up and down. "I did nothing."

Grave was taken aback. "No, of course not."

"Then why are you here?"

Grave nodded in Crab Cake Johnny's direction. "To check up on my friend here."

The man squinted at him. "How do you know Crab Cake Johnny?"

Crab Cake Johnny finally spoke up. "Leave him alone, Papa Joe. The girl, my daughter, sucker punched me, and they brought me here for a look-see at the damage she caused. The little bitch."

Grave grabbed Salamander just in time and held her tight until her body relaxed. "So, you're the famous Papa Joe?"

"I am, and what's it to you?"

"Well," said Grave, "that remains to be seen."

23

Charlize and Smithers arrived at the hospital ten minutes after Grave's drone call, just as Grave and Salamander were leaving. Grave had learned nothing from Papa Joe and very little from Crab Cake Johnny, the little amounting to no more than a grudging promise from Johnny to "check around" and see what he could see.

"Papa Joe is all yours," said Grave, "but he doesn't seem inclined to talk."

"Well, we'll just see about that," said Charlize. She turned to Smithers. "Let's go."

Grave watched them climb the steps to the hospital door and then turned to Salamander. "You've had quite a first day."

She shrugged. "We're done?"

"Till morning, yes. Can I offer you dinner at my place?"

She squinted at him.

"No, no," he said. "Just dinner. I have a housekeeper who fancies himself a chef, even though all the credit goes to our synthesizer."

She shook her head. "I didn't come to Earth for synthesizer food. I think I'll check out the boardwalk. Do some shopping—I want to get out of this uniform—and then maybe some crabs, oysters, and a local beer."

"That sounds good. There's a new place on the boardwalk, Ollie's Oysters, which is really quite good."

"Thanks, I'll check them out." She shifted back and forth on her feet. "So, can I go now?"

"Yes, of course," said Grave, moving to the side to give her a straight shot at her hovercycle. "Be careful out there."

She wasted no time jumping on the cycle and zooming away. Grave watched her go with a sense of wonder and relief.

What a pistol, he thought. *I don't know whether this planet is ready for you, but welcome, little girl.*

He walked slowly to his Austin Healy Sprite, not sure what he should do next. He could go home, have a glass of Duct Tape Chardonnay and a light dinner, and then call it a day. Or he could drive to the cemetery and see if Victoria knew anything about the recently deceased young women.

He looked at his watch and then nodded to himself. *The cemetery it is.*

24

Grave had hoped to arrive before the Crab Cove Cemetery's daily Death Parade, a new feature involving Cinema Floats that honored the lives of the recently deceased while providing Advertising Floats for local businesses, all the floats led around the cemetery by the brass section of the Crab Cove High School Marching Band and the school's cheerleading squad. But that was not to be.

Instead, he had to wait in the Sprite as the parade made its way up the hill past Victoria's bench. He didn't recognize any of the recently deceased men, women, and children being featured on the float screens, which was a disappointment. He was hoping to see Heather Van Hinkle up there on the screen, playing tennis and smiling at the camera.

Finally, the parade passed by and the trombones grew silent. He got out of the Sprite and walked up the hill to the bench. Victoria was there, and gave him a big smile and a little wave as he approached.

"Simon, how wonderful. It's been a while."

Grave nodded at her. "Good to see you, too, Victoria. Did you enjoy the parade?"

She shook her head. "It's a bit much, don't you think?"

Grave chuckled. "Well, isn't *everything* about this cemetery a bit much?"

"Point taken." She cocked her head. "Let me guess, Simon. Someone has been killed and you're here to find out if they've showed up here, right?"

He held his arms wide. "Guilty."

"Well, then, I have good news for you. Or at least I think I do. We have three new arrivals, and they all have pretty much the same story. They were running away from someone and then they were suddenly here. All they remember is a sudden greenish-blue flash. Odd, don't you think?"

"Wait, wait, did you say three women? Not two?"

"I thought I was pretty clear about that, Simon. Yes, three, two naked and one in a lovely yellow dress with little blue flowers, and all quite dead."

"Was there a tennis player?"

"Simon, they were naked. How would I know that?"

"Can you describe them, then? Was one a blonde? Another with darker hair?"

"Yes, and a redhead, the one in the yellow dress. One each, Simon. If I remember a previous discussion of ours, that would be like a trifecta, right."

"Sort of, yes." His thoughts immediately went to Salamander. "Did the redhead have a tattoo of a red salamander on her neck?"

Victoria put a finger to her lips, thinking, and then shook her head. "No, Simon, it was a little crab, but on her ankle. In fact, they all had the same tattoo, just in different places. How wonderfully curious. Oh, is that like a double trifecta?"

Simon took a deep breath.

"That's quite a sigh, Simon. What's up?"

He sat down on the bench next to her. "Nothing. I thought maybe I knew one of them."

"That would have been terrible."

"Yes, it would have been." He patted her on her knee. "Look, can you tell me more about the redhead? Did she say where she was when she saw this, um, flash?"

Victoria screwed up her face. "Let me see, let me see—*yes!* She was at the beach, splashing into the water."

Grave rolled his eyes. If she had made it into the water, she could have been swept out to sea. "What about names. Did they tell you their names?"

Victoria shook her head. "No, all those details are covered in Orientation, which is where they are now. Come back tomorrow, and I may be able to tell you more."

Simon nodded. "I'll leave you to it, then." He turned and started walking down the sidewalk.

"Simon, one other thing."

He stopped and looked back. "Yes?"

"Next time, come in time to watch the whole parade with me."

He smiled at her. "You got it, kid."

She gave him a smile and a wave, and disappeared.

He walked back to the Sprite, wondering what to do next. He spotted Barry hovering beside the car. "Barry, get Captain Morgan on the horn. Looks like we have another body." He paused and shook his head. "Somewhere."

25

Captain Morgan took the call, but he wasn't about to call in the Coast Guard and all his detectives and officers based on the questionable testimony of a ghost. He instructed Barry to tell Grave to just go home and get a good night's sleep. He wanted him fresh for the next morning's meeting.

Morgan's reply was about what Grave expected, and for his part, he wasn't about to spend the night combing the beaches, either. Not that he didn't trust Victoria. He did. They would find a body—eventually. And Captain Morgan was right; he did need sleep. Dealing with Kismet Salamander had been exhausting.

"Why are you rolling your eyes?" said Barry.

"I was thinking of our new detective, Salamander."

"She's a handful, isn't she?"

"You noticed?"

"Everyone noticed. Is she always going to be like that?"

Grave shrugged. "We'll see, I guess." He looked at his watch. "Come on, it's getting late. Let's go home."

Barry didn't need coaxing. He sped away without another word.

"Hey, wait for me," said Grave.

Ten minutes later, he rolled into the parking spot outside his lighthouse on the shore. And then he rolled his eyes again. His father's fiancé's hovercruiser was parked outside, too. That could only mean that Ida Notion and her drone Crystal and Jacob Grave and his drone Buddy would be inside.

"It's them," said Barry, zooming over and hovering next to Grave. "Do we have to go in?"

Grave sighed. "Yes, I'm afraid we do. Look, do me a favor and keep Crystal and Buddy out of my way."

"Your way? What about keeping them out of my way? They're both flying dolts. Old models. Old programming. No skills. Just annoying."

"I hear you. Okay, look, you can stay outside if you want, or even better, you can fly along the beach and see if you see the body of a young woman."

"It's dark."

"You have lights."

"It's scary."

"All right, suit yourself. "Hover out here if you want, but be ready to go first thing in the morning. Our meeting is at seven."

"No problem. I'll hook myself up to the charger and spend the night out here."

"Okay, then, I guess I better go inside."

"You could stay out here with me, you know."

"No, I'd better just get this over with." He looked at the front door, which seemed to be the entrance to hell now. "Have a good night."

"You, too."

Grave took a step toward the door and then turned back. "What if I sent Buddy and Crystal out here to be with you?"

Barry waggled in the air. "Don't you dare."

Grave shrugged. "Worth a try."

"Get in there and leave me alone."

"Right, right." He took the final ten steps to the door, which swung open before he could reach the knob. Ida was standing there with his Dad.

"Where have you been?" she said.

"What do you mean?"

"There's been a murder. I just know it."

Grave sighed again, the kind of sigh that suggested an exquisitely unbearable evening was about to commence, one that not even Duct Tape Chardonnay could help.

26

Grave was up with the sun, happy to have survived the previous evening with Ida Notion and his father. Ida, a sort of psychic who got everything right except the details, was certain several young women had been killed by a green "death ray" and that the murderer and his strange weapon were still in Crab Cove.

Grave's father couldn't have cared less about the murders. He'd been a detective for more than forty years and had had his fill of dastardly deeds. All he wanted to do was sit in the kitchen with Grave's simdroid manservant, a Peter Lorre lookalike named Roderick, and watch *Casablanca* on Surround Vision.

Finally, Ida had had her say and drifted off to sleep on the couch, joined by his father ten minutes later. "That *Casablanca* thing is pretty cool. Bogart is amazing, don't you think?"

Grave had mumbled agreement, climbed the stairs to his bedroom, and then climbed up to the walkway that circled the out-of-commission light. Horace, a seagull equipped with a surgically implanted neural node, which gave the bird the gifts of intelligence and speech, was perched on the rail, barely awake.

"Horace, are you awake?" said Grave.

Horace ruffled his feathers and forced his eyes wide open. "Of course, of course."

"I have a job for you."

"Oh?"

"There's a woman missing. Last seen near the beach. When it's light enough, could you fly along the shore and see if you can find her?"

"Sure, what does she look like?"

"She has red hair, but mostly she will look like a dead body. Oh, and she may be wearing a yellow dress."

"When did she disappear?"

"I'm not sure, probably yesterday or the day before, but recent."

"Then probably not bloated and stinky."

"Um."

"Never mind, if she's out there, I'll find her."

"And when you do, alert one of the Officer Larrys on the boardwalk so it can protect the crime scene, and then come to the station."

"Right, no problem."

Grave had thanked him and said good night, and then climbed back down to his bedroom. He had fallen asleep and enjoyed a dreamless night. Roderick had awakened him as instructed and laid out a fresh gray suit for the coming day.

Now he was racing through the streets of Crab Cove in his Sprite, trailed by Barry trying to keep up, the sound of gospel music waking anyone and anything within a mile. The birds of morning swarmed the ground, gobbling up the worms shocked from underground by the thumping bass.

Ten minutes later, he pulled into what looked like the last parking spot in front of the station. *Everyone else must already be here,* he thought.

He jumped out of the car and raced up the steps. And then he heard the sound of cheering coming from inside the station.

"What the—"

27

On any given day in the squad room of the Crab Cove Police there are only two reasons for cheering. Either a case has been solved or someone has brought in donuts for everyone.

The latter was in play as Grave pushed through the doors with Barry, and he knew from sad experience that he would have to move fast to have any hope of any kind of donut, let alone a chocolate one.

Officer Larrys said hello as he passed by, but he only grunted in return, so focused was he on the two open boxes of donuts beside the coffee pot, which was uncharacteristically full.

"Donuts," he said. "Donuts." He grabbed a chocolate donut—*there were six!*—and stuffed it in his mouth, waiting only a second or two before asking, "Who brought the donuts?"

Everyone gave him a puzzled look, his words' meaning lost under a mouthful of donut.

He chewed and swallowed, chewed and swallowed, and then asked again.

"Oh," said the nearest Officer Larry. "That would be Detective Salamander."

Grave picked up another donut and scanned the room for her, but he couldn't locate her. "Where is she?"

The Officer Larry pointed across the squad room to the door to Captain Morgan's office. A woman in a bright red pantsuit was standing in the doorway, talking to Captain Morgan. She seemed to know Morgan, but Grave had never seen her before.

He turned to the Officer Larry. "Who's that?"

The Officer Larry blinked. "Um, Kismet Salamander, sir."

Grave turned and squinted at the woman. "Really? She's too tall to be Salamander."

"Red, four-inch heels, sir."

"And that shoulder-length bright red hair. Salamander's is almost buzz cut and a duller ginger."

"A wig, sir. Invented around 3400 B.C., in Egypt, I believe."

"But she's so beautiful."

"Women, I am told, are notorious shape-shifters."

Grave just nodded and stuffed the donut into his mouth. "Weird."

"What did you say, sir? *Word?* What word?"

Grave chewed and swallowed, chewed and swallowed. "I said weird, *weird.*"

"Ah," said the Officer Larry. "A subjective conclusion."

"Yes, exactly," said Grave. He started to explain his *subjective conclusion* further, but a solid punch to his arm stopped him.

It was Loblolly, looking angry.

"Put your tongue back in your mouth," she said.

"What?"

"You look at her like she's a giant chocolate donut."

He knew he was doing exactly that, but he couldn't say that to his girlfriend. "No, no, it's just that she looks so *different.*"

Loblolly sighed. "All right, I'll give you that. Apparently, she bought the outfit and the wig right off a mannequin down at Ida's on the Beach. At least that's what Snoot said. She ran into her down at Hovercycle Mike's Saloon late last night."

"The hovercycle bar?"

"The very one. And she was apparently quite a hit with the Sons of Irony. Even danced on the bar. And stripped."

Grave's jaw dropped. "What?" He looked over at Salamander.

Loblolly punched him in the arm again. "Hey, you're imagining her naked now, aren't you?"

Captain Morgan saved him. "Detectives, to the conference room—*now!*"

28

Horace lifted off from the lighthouse at dawn and flew along the coast of Crab Cove, passing up every opportunity to eat fallen French-fries on the boardwalk and dropped food on the littered beach.

At first, he flew over the remote areas of the beach, where a killer might seek to hide a body, but he found nothing other than a life preserver that had washed up on the beach.

Then he decided to be more scientific about the search. He flew down the length of the boardwalk, then reversed himself and flew an overlapping pattern back down the boardwalk, with every turn getting closer and closer to the bay.

And then he saw it, a bright yellow lump atop a breakwater made of black boulders. He circled the lump, descending lower and lower with each circle, and then landed beside it.

It was a young woman with long red hair, beautiful by human standards, but very dead. She was wearing a bright yellow sundress cinched at the waist with a thin, brown leather belt, and pulled up over her naked rump. No underwear. No shoes. No jewelry. No blood.

He lifted the hair away from her face with his beak. No bruising or blood. Just pale blue eyes staring up at him, lifeless. He looked at her arms and legs. Again, no signs of a struggle. No bruises. No lacerations.

He looked at her eyes again and thought to pluck them out—they looked so juicy—but he knew Simon would be upset with him if he did. Or if any seagull did. He grasped one of her fingers with his beak and tugged her forearm over her eyes. Simon would be proud of him for that.

He started to lift off, but then stopped. There was a dark spot on her ankle. A small black crab tattoo, freshly inked.

29

Grave sat down next to Loblolly and gave her a little smile. She, in turn, rolled her eyes and wiped his mouth with a napkin.

"You and your chocolate donuts," she said.

"Um, thanks," said Grave, looking around the room.

Everyone was staring at them.

Grave frowned and turned to Captain Morgan. "Are we going to start this meeting, or what?"

Morgan smirked. He would have to have another talk with Grave and Loblolly about office romances and the need for professional behavior.

"Yes, let's do that." He scanned the room, making sure everyone was paying attention. "So, we have two bodies—"

"Three," said Grave, noting the stunned look on everyone's faces. "Um, we haven't found the third one yet, but I have it on good authority that there's a third victim out there."

"Maybe," said Morgan, frowning. "Grave here said that ghost of his gave him the information."

Salamander perked up. "Ghost?"

"Yes," said Grave. "Her name is Victoria Skunkford. Ten years old, died in the mid-1700s, now works as a greeter at the Crab Cove Cinema Cemetery."

"For real?" said Salamander. "I mean, we have ghosts on Mars, too—mostly dead miners—but no little girls."

Grave nodded. "I'll take you to see her if you want."

Morgan rapped his knuckles on the table. "Can we keep on topic, please?"

"Of course," said Grave. "So, the third victim is also young, has red hair and the same crab tattoo, but on her ankle. Oh, and according to Victoria, she's wearing a yellow dress with little blue flowers."

"Oh," said Salamander. "I saw one of those last night, at a dress shop on the boardwalk. Not for me. Too girly-girly."

"Right," said Morgan, pumping out a breath in frustration. "Now, if you don't mind, let's get back to the bodies we *know*."

"No," said Loblolly. "Victoria has been right before. We should call out the coastguard right away."

"That may not be necessary," said Grave. "I have Horace on the case."

"Horace, who's Horace?" said Salamander.

Grave paused, not knowing exactly what to say.

Snoot helped him out. "A seagull."

"That talks," said Loblolly.

"Yes," said Grave. "He has a neural node implant that has given him above-average intelligence and the gift of speech."

"Freaky," said Salamander. "I've heard of neural nodes—some of our scientists on Mars have them—but never one for a seagull. Can I meet him?"

There was an insistent tapping on the conference room door.

"Yes," said Grave. "Right now, I think."

Grave stood, walked to the door, and opened it, allowing Horace to fly in and land on the conference table.

"Found her," said Horace. "Down on the beach. Found an Officer Larry to protect the scene."

"Good work," said Grave.

"Didn't eat her eyeballs."

"Even better."

Morgan waved his arms in the air, trying to indicate that everyone should rise from their chairs with some urgency. "Come on, people, let's go."

"Wait," said God. "I thought we were going to watch the synched CCTV tapes."

Morgan shook his head. "We will, but not now. Right now I want all eyes on the new crime scene."

30

Polk kneeled next to the body and hummed to himself as he went through his routine on-scene examination, looking for obvious signs of death and ruminating about time of death. The others stood as close as they could, each balancing on a different rock as the waves crashed into the barrier. Horace soared overhead, watching the action below, as did Barry and the other drones: Blunt's Object, Loblolly's Sparky, Snoot's Midnight, and Morgan's Rum.

Finally, Polk stood up and turned to Morgan. "If I had to guess—and you know how much I hate to guess, Henry—I'd say this young woman died first, but not by much, maybe just minutes. There are no obvious signs of death, so I'll have to take her back and see what's what. She has sand between her toes and a few cuts on her soles from shells, so I'd say, like the others, she was fleeing her attacker. No jewelry, though there are signs of piercings. Several in each ear and what looks like a nose piercing, as well as one in her bellybutton. And of course, the crab tattoo, which looks fairly fresh to me. The odd thing—or one of many odd things—is that she's wearing a dress while the others were both nude."

Salamander leaped from her rock to one closer to Morgan and Polk. "It's the belt. Some buckles are absolutely insanely difficult to undo. And that one looks like a tough nut to crack."

"Makes sense," said Morgan.

Charlize spoke up. "And if he did try to take the belt off, there's a good chance we can pull some prints."

"Exactly," said Salamander.

"And after we test for prints," said Snoot, "let's see just how difficult it is to open that belt."

"What are you thinking?" said Loblolly.

"I'm thinking if the belt is actually difficult to open, fine. But if it's easy, then maybe we're dealing with a killer with a disability. A problem with one of their hands perhaps."

"Or both hands," said Morgan.

"Or an arm," said Smithers.

"Or both arms," said Blunt.

"Or maybe he's missing an arm," said Grave.

Morgan rolled his eyes. "Grave, it's possible, but don't tell me we're chasing a one-armed man."

"But it's possible," said Grave.

"On the other hand," said God. "Maybe the guy is just clumsy. I know a few people who have a heck of a time opening those plastic bags at the grocery store."

Polk held both arms up. "Stop!" He turned to Morgan. "Henry, I think we've said enough about the damned belt. I'll have my guys take prints and then we'll just see what's what. Okay?"

Morgan nodded. "Okay." He turned to the others. "Anything else before we go back to the station?"

"Yes," said Salamander. "Two things. First, where are their drones? They should stay close to their owners, but they're nowhere to be seen."

"Good point," said Morgan. "And two?"

"Two, where's the jewelry? Are we dealing with robbery?"

"Or trophies?" said Charlize.

"Yes, exactly," said Salamander.

"I can handle the drones," said Blunt. He turned to Salamander. "My wife works at Ramrod Robotics, where most of the drones are built. They keep a registry and monitor GPS locations of all the drones they've built. Part of their service."

"That's fine for Van Hinkle," said Grave. "But we don't have the names for the other victims."

Morgan nodded. "We'll have to check with Missing Persons and try to get matches for the other two. Loblolly, Snoot, can you guys handle that?"

Both looked at each other and nodded.

"We'll get right on it," said Loblolly.

"Before you do that," said Morgan, "let's get back to the station. I want all of you to see the synched CCTV tapes." He turned to Polk. "Let us know about the belt and anything else revealed by the autopsy."

Polk gave him a quick nod, then turned back to the body.

"All right, people," said Morgan, "let's get back to the station."

31

God rolled the CCTV tape forward and backward over and over, showing the greenish-blue flash again and again as everyone looked on in wonderment. "So that's it. She's running and then there's that flash and she goes down like a powerless drone."

Salamander raised her hand. "I know what that is. I've used it myself on Mars. It's a portal. Radiation is a big problem on Mars, so we use it to go from one place to another, do our work, and then return without being exposed at all."

"Why is it that color?" said Grave.

"Good question. That doesn't happen on Mars, but here, when the portal opens, free electrons are released and react with the oxygen in your atmosphere, causing that flash of color."

"I don't get it," said Loblolly. "If it's just a flash, how can you get anything done? It's there for an instant, and then it's gone. Poof."

"To an observer, yes," said Salamander. "To the worker within the portal, time in effect stands still. I could work for hours within that flash. A great boon to productivity."

"Wow," said Morgan. "But who would have access to that technology here?"

Salamander shook her head. "No one. It's strictly regulated for use on Mars."

Morgan nodded. "So it would have to be stolen."

"Exactly. Someone from Mars brought it here. Or more likely, someone stole the design and built it here."

"To kill women?"

Salamander shrugged. "Maybe, but it's more likely the three women are collateral damage. They might have just seen something they shouldn't have seen."

Snoot raised her hand. "Could someone on Mars, um, beam down to Earth using this technology?"

Salamander shook her head. "No, it only has a range of a five miles on Mars, and here, with your thicker atmosphere, my guess is that the range is reduced to just a couple of miles. The hope is to eventually make it powerful enough to use between Mars and Earth, but the technology is just not there yet. That's good news for us. The machine is somewhere in a two mile radius of Skunk 'n Donuts."

"How big a machine are we talking about?" said Charlize.

Salamander screwed up her face. "Um, it's basically a brushed aluminum cylinder, seven feet high and four feet in diameter, with a door."

"So pretty hard to hide," said Morgan.

"It's big, yes," said Salamander, "but it's easy enough to hide in a building or even in a truck. And it's relatively light. Two strong men could pick it up."

"Could it be disguised as a tanker truck?" said Smithers.

Salamander shook her head. "No, you can only use it when the cylinder is vertical. It would have to be a large 18-wheeler."

"And if it's in a building," said Grave, "it would have to be a building with doors wider than four feet."

"Warehouses or other buildings with loading docks," said Charlize.

"Or mansions with double doors," said Smithers.

Morgan rubbed a hand across his bald head. "A lot of possibilities. Look, we'll find it, but first I want God to finish his presentation." He turned to God. "All yours, Freeman."

"Okay, take a look at this." He punched a few buttons on the synching console and a clip of Heather Van Hinkle running backwards came on. She ran toward the boardwalk and then turned onto the boardwalk, heading south. God slowed things down. "Watch carefully."

He slowed it down further. Now Van Hinkle appeared to be walking backwards. God stopped the tape again. "Here it is. Watch the right of the screen. Suddenly there was a second young woman.

"The brunette," said Grave. "They're running together."

"Yes," said God. "Now watch this." God let the tape run backwards till the two women disappeared from view. "They're coming from the darkness of the beach."

"Wow, they look like they're screaming," said Loblolly.

"They saw something terrifying," said Grave.

"Probably the flash associated with the death of the woman in the yellow dress."

"And they realized that they were seen and were in danger."

"So they run," said Blunt. "One to the donut shop and the other down the boardwalk toward Papa Joe's."

"Exactly," said God. "They were witnesses."

Morgan rubbed his head again. "That moment when they emerge from the darkness. Does it correlate with the location of the redhead on the rocks?"

"Yes," said God.

"And do we have any CCTV coverage of the beach there?"

"Unfortunately, no," said God.

"I wonder," said Grave. "Was the flash intended for the woman in the yellow dress, or was she just collateral damage like the other two? Saw something she shouldn't have."

"It sounds like it to me," said Salamander. "I mean, why would someone go to all the trouble of stealing the portal just to kill three women? Why not just shoot them or something. No, the portal was brought here for some other purpose. But what?"

Morgan ran his hand over his bald head again, this time more vigorously. Grave and the others knew the mannerism would be followed by a pronouncement.

"Okay," said Morgan. "This is what we're going to do."

"No, wait," said God. "One more thing." He walked to the conference room door and admitted an Officer Larry carrying a bucket. The officer walked in and dumped its contents, an array of sandy jewelry—rings, earrings, bracelets, and necklaces—spilling across the table.

"I had a squad of Officer Larrys use metal detectors to comb the beach. We also picked up a few pieces of jewelry from local beachcombers."

"Good work," said Morgan, giving his head another brief rub. "Well now, that adds another tool to our tool box. Let's get pics of all these so we can show them to friends and relatives. Maybe we'll find a match that leads to a name for those other two women." He frowned. "Where was I?"

"You were about to tell us all what to do," said Grave.

"Ah, yes. Okay, people, listen up."

32

Sergeant Blunt was tasked with finding the victims' drones. Loblolly and Snoot were to go through missing person reports and try to find a match for the unidentified victims. Charlize and Smithers-Watson were sent to the country club to continue interviews with friends, family, and associates of Heather Van Hinkle. As usual, Captain Morgan would "hold down the fort."

That left Grave, Salamander, God, and a team of ten Officer Larrys to find the portal. Grave sent God and the Larrys to the Crab Cove Industrial Park to search more than twenty warehouses with loading docks, as well as any 18-wheelers in the park. Grave and Salamander would start their search at Dolly's Robo Truck Stop.

Dolly's had been serving and servicing trucks and their drivers for more than fifty years, and had seen the rough transition from gas to electric vehicles and from human to simdroid drivers and autonomous trucks. Now only a few aging human drivers remained, most working for Acme Freight, a company that grudgingly made the transition to electric—it just made economic sense—but balked at the move to nonhuman drivers.

Grave had been to Dolly's once before, looking for a fugitive, so he knew the best place to start was with Dolly herself.

She grunted when she saw them walk in. "Oh, my dear god, what now, Grave?"

Dolly Bigolly was a round woman, as wide as she was tall, with short gray hair and a frown surrounded by wrinkles that flashed like lightning when she spoke. Her blunt pig nose sat between two rheumy blue eyes, one of which wandered in different directions. It was hard to tell what she was looking at from her permanent location in a massive recliner that had molded itself to her body over the years. Her drone Loopy sat on the back of the chair, its eyes squinting at Salamander.

"Not looking for a fugitive this time, Dolly," said Grave.

Dolly joined Loopy in the squint fest aimed at Salamander. "Who's this?"

"I'm Detective Kismet Salamander."

"Nice pantsuit. Red becomes you."

"Thank you." She looked at Grave, raising her eyebrows to get him to continue.

He caught the look. "Oh, yes. Dolly, we're here looking for a cylinder."

"A what?"

"Cylinder," said Salamander. "Made of aluminum, and big. About eight feet high and four feet in diameter. We suspect it may be on one of the trucks here."

Dolly cocked her head. "I like your eyes, too. I forget what that's called when you have eyes like that."

"It's called heterochromia, a genetic condition that causes the irises to be different colors. Rare on Earth but very common among Martians. They think it may be caused by the high levels of radiation there, as well as a relatively limited gene pool."

Dolly's eyes widened. "So you're from *Mars?*"

"Yes, she is," said Grave. "Helping us with our investigation."

"So *Mars* is involved?"

"Yes," said Salamander, "but let's get back to the question."

Dolly looked confused. "And what question was that?"

"The cylinder. Have you seen the cylinder?"

Dolly smirked. "I don't remember that question, but as you can see, I'm not one to wander around my truck stop looking for cylinders of *any* kind."

"Yes, sorry," said Salamander.

"Don't be sorry, dearie. I make a good living from this chair."

"I didn't mean to—

"No, I know you didn't, dearie." She looked at Grave, or at least one of her eyes did. The other seemed to be looking Salamander up and down like she was a fine morsel. "You can look around all you want, talk to anyone you want. Just make it quick."

Grave nodded. "Any Acme trucks in the lot?"

She nodded back. "Six or so, over at the north end—they don't like to mix with the other trucks."

"We'll head over there, then. Thank you for your time."

"No problem, Grave." She looked at Salamander. "You come back and see me, you hear. I'd like to learn more about Mars—and you."

Salamander gave her a quick nod and turned for the door. "You coming, Grave?"

He was. He turned and headed for the door.

"And you, Grave," Dolly said. "You look much older standing next to her. Maybe you should consider getting some work done."

Grave turned back and gave her a weak smile. "Thank you, thank you very much."

As they left, she began to chuckle, the wrinkles on her face dancing.

33

God and the Larrys searched every warehouse and hovertruck at the industrial park, and found nothing. Then they moved on to the boardwalk and searched the storage rooms of every business up and down the boardwalk save one—Papa Joe's, which was locked up tight—and found nothing, absolutely nothing. He would report the problem with Papa Joe's to Morgan. They'd have to get a warrant, if necessary.

The question now was, should they move on to the mansions on the hill? It was already mid-afternoon, and searching the mansions would be a slow process.

God sat down on a bench looking out at the bay and pondered the question. As usual, a steady stream of freighters passed by in both directions, coming from and going to New Baltimore, forty miles west of the now submerged Baltimore. There was civilian traffic as well: sailing boats, speedboats, fishing boats, crab boats, oyster boats, and ten or more autonomous cargo boats that handled local commerce.

God thought and thought. God watched the ship traffic. He thought more and more. More ships and boats passed by. And then like many gods, he had a revelation, the answer to his question hitting him like a sudden surge of power at his recharging station.

He would not go to the mansions.

He leaped up and shouted at the other Larrys. "Back to the station!"

34

Loblolly and Snoot sat in front of the Global Missing Persons Identifier and listened to the strange sounds coming from the machine, which seemed to match the clangs and dings and crunches and gnashings of an MRI machine.

They had uploaded images of the two women's faces, as well as images for more than a hundred pieces of jewelry, and punched the start button, initiating a cacophonous search of missing person files worldwide.

"How long is this going to take?" said Loblolly.

"It could be minutes if the missing person is local, or hours—even days—if the missing person is from another country."

"But it will stop when it finds a match, right?"

"Yes, if we're lucky, the GMPI will find a match based on their faces; if not, it will turn to the jewelry, and that could create a large number of false positives."

"I'm hoping for faces."

"Me, too, I want to get out there and help with the search for that portal cylinder."

They settled back in their chairs and listened. Sometimes a series of clanks and whistles and trills would have them leaning forward, hoping for a result, but the machine would suddenly go quiet, clanks coming less often.

They waited and waited. Minutes passed, and then an hour.

"Jeez," said Loblolly, "this is taking a long time."

"Not all that long," said the GMPI. "Believe me, I've had cases that took weeks."

Loblolly was stunned. It had a woman's voice and a decidedly English accent. "You can talk?"

"Of course I can talk," it said. "My programmer insisted on it. And I can sing, too. Something to take your minds off the delay, if you like."

"That won't be necessary," said Snoot. "Just tell us where you are now in your search."

"Nothing in Crab Cove or the Greater Crabopolis, so I've spread the search north to New Philadelphia, west to Cumberland, and south to New Norfolk."

"What's with all the clanks?" said Loblolly. "I mean, how will we know when you've found a match?"

"Ah, good question," it said. "If it's a sort-of match, there will be a bell. If it's a good match, there will be a whistle, and if it's an excellent match, I will launch into song."

"What song?"

"I don't know, it's random. Anything from New Hillbilly to Quantum Jazz, to Queen covers. Sometimes even classical music."

"Um, okay," said Loblolly. "I guess we'd better let you get back to work, then."

"Okay," it said. "Talk to you soon, I hope." Its voice was replaced by renewed clangs, knocks, and bangs.

"She seems nice," said Loblolly.

Snoot gave her a funny look.

"What?" said Loblolly.

"It's a machine, Polly. A *machine.*"

Loblolly slumped back in her chair. As soon as her back hit the chair, the GMPI launched into a bad, off-key cover of Queen's "Bohemian Rhapsody."

Snoot let it sing for a few seconds, then shouted, "Stop!"

The GMPI stopped singing and its regular voice came back. "What? Why? Don't you like my singing?"

Snoot rolled her eyes, and lied. "Your singing is fine, but we need the match."

It sighed. "As you wish. Watch the screen. Your match is coming up in two point six seconds."

As predicted, the screen lit up, showing two photos that matched and four lines of data:

Judy DuPree
Age 23
New Philadelphia
Contact: Sergeant Wanda Willis, Precinct Six

"Great," said Loblolly. "It's the victim that was found under the boardwalk."

"What about the other one?" said Snoot.

"Nothing yet," said the GMPI. "Expanding my search. Please stand by." It clanked once, followed by a sound that resembled corn popping.

Snoot sighed. "I hope this doesn't take too much longer."

"Me, too," said Loblolly. "But let's give the captain a heads up."

"Right," said Snoot. "You go do that, and I'll contact this Wanda Willis."

"Right, and then we need to give Charlize and Smithers a heads up—might help them in their interviews."

"And give Blunt a call."

"Oh right, his search for the drones."

"Are you sure you don't want to hear me sing some more?" said the GMPI.

Snoot and Loblolly gave it a quick and emphatic, "Yes!"

35

By late afternoon Charlize and Smithers had exhausted every avenue of discussion with Van Hinkle's father, her coach Larry Flan, the tournament director Jacky Pompo, the club director Manley Morris, and fifteen of her competitors, and learned nothing.

Sally Fifth, the concierge, was escorting them out when they received the call about Judy Dupree, as well as a better picture of her, not one of a face distorted by death.

Fifth was sallying forth as quickly as she could on her high heels, so Charlize had to pursue her and grab her by the arm.

"Wait, we have new information," said Charlize.

Fifth gave her a confused look. "What? What do you mean?"

"I mean we have to talk to everyone again."

"But you've spent *hours*—"

"And it will only take a few minutes more. Gather them all in the conference room, and we'll talk to them all at once."

Fifth rolled her eyes. "Really?"

"Yes, really."

Fifth sighed. "You people. You're screwing up this tournament."

Charlize ignored the comment. "Do it."

Fifth set her mouth in a deep sneer and clacked away down the hall toward the club offices.

Charlize turned to Smithers. "Let's get back to the conference room."

Fifteen minutes later Fifth clacked in, followed by all the others, each and every one of them looking exasperated by the process.

Charlize wasted no time. "Form a line along that far wall, and we'll be out of here in two minutes."

They complied more quickly than Charlize expected, as if they were soldiers waiting for their commander to pass in review.

"Very good," said Charlize. "Now then, we have a name for the second victim. Her name is Judy Dupree."

The name prompted a squeak from one of the players, who stepped out of line and held up her hand.

"Yes?" said Charlize. "Um, I'm sorry, I've forgotten your name."

"Viv Val."

"Right, right, so?"

"I know her. She was kind of a groupie. Pretty annoying, but Heather befriended her."

"Befriended?" said Charlize.

The girl looked up and down the line nervously. "Well, more than friends, really."

The other players nodded, Jacky Pompo slapped his head, Manley Morris shrugged, Sally Fifth continued her fixed sneer, and Koos Van Hinkle stared straight ahead, his face struggling to fix itself into the blank stare that he was trying to achieve.

36

Sergeant Barry Blunt's wife, June, looked at the second name, the new one. "Judy Dupree, huh?"

"Yes, from New Philadelphia."

"Have an address?"

"Not yet."

"Okay, let's see what we can get anyway."

They had already entered the data for Heather Van Hinkle and come up with a drone name of Matchy, a reference to Heather's profession as a professional tennis player. Then June had entered the GPS identifier for Matchy and waited for the computer to find the drone's current GPS coordinates. The results were as confusing as they were seemingly impossible. June thought she or the computer had made a mistake, and she was about to rerun the data when the call came in with Judy Dupree's information.

"Let's hope we get better results with this one. If not, I may have to recalibrate the machine or put in a call to GPS Central."

"Right," said Blunt.

"Okay," said June. "Here we go." She clacked the keys on the keyboard and hit enter. The computer came back with the drone name Doody. "Okay, so Judy and Doody, huh. Priceless."

"And where is it?" said Blunt.

"We'll see." She entered the drone identifier data and waited for the computer to do its work again.

A map of the Greater Crabopolis came on the screen and then zoomed in on a specific GPS location.

June pointed at a spot on the screen. "The same place as Van Hinkle's."

"But that's just not possible," said Blunt.

June waggled her head. "Unless . . ."

"Oh, no," said Blunt, "you can't seriously be suggesting that . . ."

"Yes, it's possible."

Blunt shook his head.

"You want me to run them again?" said June.

"No, no, I think it's accurate, and if it is . . ."

"We've got big problems, right here in River City."

Blunt nodded. "I better get back to the station."

"And fast."

37

Salamander could not stop shaking her head as they walked away from the Acme Trucking area of the lot. "This has been a complete waste of time. Dolly, the truckers at Acme, the search of the rest of those damned trucks, all of it."

"Not a waste," said Grave. "We've just eliminated one of the possibilities. Remember, God is out there searching, too."

"Yes, yes," said Salamander, "but it's totally frustrating."

"Just part of the job. Surely you run into this on Mars."

"Not really. There's not too many places to hide and if you go beyond those places, you're dead."

"All right, we've had a bad day. Let's head back to the station." He looked at his watch. "It's a bit early, but we should still go."

"No, I have a better idea."

"Oh?"

"Let's go to that cemetery of yours. I've never seen a cemetery before."

Grave nodded. "Okay, so it's on your bucket list?"

"Bucket list? What's that?"

Grave stopped in his tracks. "You've never heard of a bucket list?"

"When it comes to this planet, I haven't heard a lot or seen a lot."

"A bucket list is a list of things you want to do before you die."

She brightened. "Oh, you mean a crater list."

"Um, I guess. So do you have a crater list?"

"When it comes to Earth, yes, I do."

"Like dancing on a bar?"

She laughed. "Snoot told you? That little bitch."

"Yes she did, and once you get to know her, you won't be calling her that."

"Maybe. Anyway, yes, that was on my list, and I managed to check off quite a few other things last night."

"Oh, like what?"

She shook her head. "Oh, no, my crater list is quite secret."

"What, you can't tell me anything?"

"Okay, a couple. I went to a bar, check. I danced on a bar, check. With a biker, check. Who kissed me, check. And then I ran naked along the beach under a full moon."

"Whoa," said Grave.

"Until an Officer Larry caught me and gave me a warning about such behavior."

"Why running naked?"

"Think about it, old man. You're either in a uniform all day or a confining spacesuit. The world closes in on you, you get claustrophobic. So tossing all that aside, running naked and free in a warm breeze, is a delight not to be missed."

"But you must have had something you could do to let off a little steam."

Salamander snorted. "Well, there was the occasional prisoner delivery to the penal colony on Phobos, and maybe you could count Deimos Disney."

"Disney?"

"Yeah, a theme park built on Deimos. Virtual reality pods. Gravity tube rollercoasters, that kind of thing. But once you've done Disney, you've pretty much done Disney, except maybe for MOC."

Grave squinted at her. "And that's . . ."

"Mickey's Orbital Casino, but I'm still too young to go there. And the Mars Orbital Hilton is pretty much your standard boring hotel."

"Oh." Grave didn't know what else to say. "Well, then, a cemetery may be just the thing to do next."

38

Morgan sat in his high-backed executive chair and wondered what to do next. He had shuffled all the papers he could shuffle. He had dusted all his Captain Morgan Rum tchotchkes. He had even taken a cloth to the tips of his black patent leather shoes. He had drummed his fingers on the desk, trying his best to emulate the drum rolls of marching bands. And he had puffed out sigh after sigh.

So he was more than happy to see the Officer Larry approaching his desk. Officer Larrys are all trained to knock on his door, but Morgan waved him in before a knock was even possible.

"What is it?"

"The prisoner, sir."

Morgan blinked. He had forgotten all about Wanda Orville. "Oh, oh, what about her?"

"She wants to talk with you. A complaint, I think."

Morgan rubbed his bald head, and nodded. "Okay, I'll go see her."

"Would you like me to come, too?"

"No, me and Rum will handle it."

The Officer Larry nodded and left.

Morgan nodded at his drone. "Let's go."

The small, two-cell jail was located on the basement level, and to Morgan's mind, always smelled of sweat, urine, and the grease of a thousand never-finished meals.

Wanda Orville was waiting for him, her hands grasping the bars at the front of the cell. "You need to get me out of this shithole."

Morgan tried his best I-don't-give-a-shit smile coupled with a similar shrug. "It's out of my hands. Waiting for the feds to come pick you up."

She returned his smile with a deep, almost sincere pouting frown. "Captain, captain, *please*. This place is worse than the penal colony on Phobos."

Morgan smirked. "It is what it is, lady. Now, unless you have something else to say to me, I—"

There was a greenish-blue flash, and she was gone.

39

Grave tried to keep up with Salamander, but her hovercycle was just too fast for the Sprite and much faster than his drone Barry, who lagged well behind. How Salamander even found the cemetery was a mystery to Grave, but there she was, waiting in the parking lot, shaking her head and staring at her watch.

"You are slow, old man."

He looked at her and smiled. "Well, at least I didn't lose a wig."

She put both hands on her head, and rolled her eyes. "It was scratchy, anyway."

"Frankly, you look better without it."

She cocked her head. "Okay, old man."

"Do you have to call me that?"

She shrugged. "No."

"How about *Simon*?"

"That will work, and you can call me *Kismet*, but never *Kiz*."

"Why is that?"

"My father."

Grave didn't pursue it further, and fortunately Barry arrived to provide a distraction. Grave looked at him and laughed. "You realize you're wearing Kismet's wig, right?"

"Of course," said Barry. "I could barely see. It was scary."

"So give it back to her."

"No," said Kismet. "It looks better on him."

Grave chuckled. "Barry, leave it on the seat of her hovercycle. We have a cemetery to see."

Grave gave her the grand tour, showing her the various sections, each with its own theme, and the many gravesite video and hologram displays along the way. They had missed the daily parade, but his description of it had her laughing out loud. "I just can't believe this place."

"Anything like it on Mars?"

She shook her head. "Oh, my, no. The dead go into what we call a digester, where their bodies are dissolved into a slurry that is eventually distilled into medicines and fertilizer. What's left goes into building blocks. Nothing is wasted."

Grave stopped in his tracks. "Really?"

"Yes, it's too dangerous to dig in the soil, anyway. Full of deadly perchlorates. And we don't have the technology up there yet to consider cremation."

"But you have a service, a ceremony, right?"

"Some do, but I've never been to one." She looked at the path leading up the hill, where she could see a young girl in a gingham dress. "Is that her? Your *ghost?*"

Grave looked surprised. "You can see her?"

"Clearly. Come on, I have some questions for her."

Grave tried to keep up, and just managed to reach Victoria first. "Victoria, I'd like you to meet Detective Kismet Salamander. She's from Mars."

"Oh, my," said Victoria. "How wonderful. I sometimes see it in the night sky. You must tell me everything about it."

"I'd be happy to do that, but first I have a few questions."

"About those three women?"

"For starters. I'm also curious about you and how you came to be here as a ghost."

"Of course," said Victoria. She pointed down the path. "But I think we have a visitor."

They turned to look down the path. Barry was flying up the hill, still wearing the wig. "We need to get back to the station, fast. The prisoner, Wanda Orville, has disappeared."

"Escaped?" said Grave.

"No," said Barry, "*vanished*, in a greenish-blue flash."

40

Captain Morgan explained as calmly as he could what had happened in the cells below, but his voice still had a slight quaver as he wrapped up. "It was amazing really. And scary."

Salamander nodded. "I bet. So, my take on this is that we will not find her body at some point. No, I think she is part of this scheme. Maybe not part of the murders, but part of the scheme to bring the portal technology here. She was on Mars for quite some time before she was apprehended. Then she spent months in the penal colony on Phobos, where she came into contact with the worst criminals of Mars. No, this was a rescue, not an attack."

Jeremy Polk stood up and cleared his throat. "I'd like to add something here. The third victim, who was actually the first victim, was from Mars."

Salamander gasped. "What?"

"Indeed. She has an identifying tattoo just behind her ear, just as you do, Salamander."

Salamander reached for her neck, then pulled her hand down. "So you have the number. Good. We can track her down easily. I'll just need space comms, and I know exactly who to call."

Morgan nodded. "Great, do that right after the meeting." He turned to Polk. "Anything else from the autopsy?"

"Pretty straightforward. She was injected with a poison, the same poison that killed Van Hinkle. But with a twist. She had been subdued with chloroform before the injection."

"A planned murder, then," said Charlize. "Some conflict or disagreement, perhaps. A falling out."

Grave raised his hand. "So, at least two Martians and the beautiful Wanda Orville involved." He turned to Salamander. "Are you sure about the range of the portal device? Could all this be coming directly from Mars?"

Salamander frowned. "No, it's a short-range device. It's here, on Earth, somewhere."

"Speaking of that," said Morgan. "Am I correct in assuming you had no luck finding it?"

Grave nodded. "We came up empty."

God smiled. "We came up empty, too, but then I had a thought. It's not in a truck or hidden in a warehouse, it's on a ship."

"I agree," said Sergeant Blunt. "June and I tracked down the drones of the two women, and they are currently a mile off the coast and thirty feet deep."

Morgan blinked. "A submarine?" He glanced over at Grave. "Are we talking about Chester Clink, the serial killer?"

Salamander spoke up. "I don't know who that is, or why you're all looking at each other like someone broke wind, but let's get real. Is there really a submarine out there with a hatch four feet in diameter?"

"No," said Charlize. "I believe the current hatch dimension on navy submarines is thirty inches, and most private submarines are even smaller than that."

"But we can't rule out subs yet," said Snoot. "Maybe the device is attached to the sub, not in the sub."

"Or maybe the device is being towed by a surface ship," said Loblolly.

Morgan held up a hand. "Whoa. All of those are possibilities, but we do know it's out there in the water, and thanks to June, we know exactly where the drones are. If we're lucky, the device is in the same place." He turned to Blunt. "Can we track it from June's office?"

"Yes, no problem."

"Okay, you and Grave head on back to June's and relay the position to us. I'll coordinate with the Coast Guard."

"Sounds good," said Grave.

"Now," said Morgan, "before we leave, a couple of things." He pointed at Salamander. "Find out who that woman is and any possible links to other Martians who might have knowledge of the device."

She nodded. "No problem."

"Now, all of you, do you agree with me that the first two victims, Van Hinkle and Dupree, are just collateral damage to a larger scheme?"

Everyone nodded, then Charlize spoke up. "All of our interviews suggest just that."

"Then we'll put that part of the investigation on hold and focus on finding the device. Agreed?"

Everyone nodded.

"Okay, Grave and Blunt, off you go." He turned to the others. "The rest of you stand by while I arrange things with the coast guard."

"What about me?" said God. "You'll need God's help, right."

Morgan rolled his eyes. "Don't worry, Freeman. There's always something for God to do."

41

Bells rang. Whistles blew. Men ran. Officers shouted. Engines revved and roared. Water spewed. Waves waved. Wakes woke, surged, and dissipated. And the ships of the coast guard pursued and boarded the *Emerald Sea*, a hoverfreighter out of New Liverpool. The drones of Heather Van Hinkle and Judy Dupree were pulled up on lines that had been tied to the stern of the ship. The captain of the *Emerald Sea* shrugged and lifted his hands palms up. He had no idea where the drones came from. The ship was searched up and down and side to side, and they found . . .

Nothing.

Captain Henry Morgan sat at the head of the conference table. He had been silent for quite some time, but then offered all present a sigh for the ages, its force lifting Polly Loblolly's hair at the other end of the table. "Okay, people, let's go over what we know about that damned portal device."

"We know its dimensions," said Snoot.

"We know the four places where it appeared," said Loblolly, adjusting her hair.

"We know that Wanda Orville was taken by it," said Sergeant Blunt.

"We now know the name of the victim found on the breakwater," said Salamander. "She's Phoebe Denali, age 21, a research scientist who interestingly was working on the prototype of a replacement portal device, one said to have a longer range."

"That *is* interesting," said Morgan. "What else?"

"Well," said Grave, "we know a couple of things we don't know."

"Go on," said Morgan.

"We don't know where it is, and we don't know who's behind it all."

Morgan nodded. "I think we'll find the latter when we find the former." He looked around the room. "As to the latter, we at least need to do something. What do we know about the portal? Yes, we have the research scientist's name. But who actually builds the portal device on Mars?"

Salamander raised her hand. "Um, I asked that question when I talked to the authorities on Mars. It's made right here in Crab Cove, at a facility called C3."

Grave sat up in his seat. "Wait, what? C3 is Wanda Orville's company. They used to make drones."

"Wow," said Morgan. "Why don't you and Blunt and Salamander check them out once we break up?"

"Will do," said Grave. Salamander gave him a quick smile and nodded her head.

"Now, as to the former," said Morgan, "let's chart the location of every truck and ship within a five mile radius at the approximate time of the murders and the abduction, say a plus/minus of half an hour each way. Then let's scan for a match in both sets of data."

"Wow," said Charlize, "that's what I was going to suggest."

"And I," said Smithers.

"We can work on that," said Charlize.

"Good," said Morgan.

"What about Loblolly and me?" said Snoot.

"Hmm," said Morgan. "Let me think." Morgan tapped his fingers on the table and looked at the ceiling. Not a single idea dropped into his head. "Well, um . . ."

"We could help Charlize, or even go with Grave," said Snoot.

The captain continued staring at the ceiling. "Well, um . . ."

God raised his hand. "Sir, there's something we've all forgot about. Something important."

"Like what?"

God pointed at the ceiling.

"The ceiling?"

God rolled his eyes and jabbed his finger at the ceiling.

"What, Heaven?"

"No," said God. "The air above us. Filled with cargo planes, freighter drones, helicopters, and those new dirigibles."

Morgan sighed.

Loblolly, alarmed, reached for her hair.

42

Blunt and Salamander were waiting for him when he arrived in the parking lot of C3 Corporation, followed by Barry, who seemed to be pixilated.

"What's up with you?" said Grave, getting out of the Sprite and waving to the others.

Barry made a mechanical giggling sound. "Dolores, of course."

"Oh," said Grave, "the dreamy drone?"

"Exactly," said Barry.

Dolores was the company's welcoming drone, a shimmering, rotorless vision in chrome who knew everything about the history of the company and its array of products, from its early robotic vacuum cleaners to its cellphones to its rotorless drones, of which she was the company's exemplar.

But that was three years ago now.

Grave turned to Salamander. "Some building, huh?"

Salamander shook her head, and laughed. "It's no building. It's a construction in glass and chrome, a geometric monstrosity."

Grave laughed. "It is that. Wait till you get inside. It's even stranger."

"*If* we can get inside," said Blunt.

"What do you mean?" said Grave.

"It's locked up tight. We knocked and knocked, but no response at all."

Grave squinted at the building. "No lights."

"Exactly," said Salamander.

"And look at the tall weeds growing through the cracks in the sidewalk," said Blunt. "This building has been abandoned, if you ask me."

Grave squinted at the building again. "Did you try the doorbell?"

They shook their heads.

"We couldn't find one," said Salamander.

"Ah," said Grave, motioning up the stairs to the glass doors. "It's made of glass, too. Hard to see."

After a few moments of confusion, Grave found the button and pushed it. A familiar voice came on.

"Hello, my name is Dolores, and I'm sorry to inform you that C3 Corporation has shuttered its operations at this building. If you would like to place a bid on these premises, please contact Crab Claw Real Estate at 301-899-7362-04. Thank you."

The message ended, and Grave blinked. "Damn!"

He turned to Barry. "Call the number and put it on speaker."

"Already on it," said Barry.

They all listened as Barry's internal phone beeped out the number, then clicked. "The number you have called is no longer in service. Please check your number and try again."

Grave sighed. "Oh, it just keeps getting better and better."

43

Salamander had only known Grave for a couple of days, so she wasn't sure whether his faraway stare was because he was contemplating the case or absently stuffing chocolate donuts in his mouth, the developing ring of chocolate already reaching his chin and his nose. Occasionally he would grunt or chew faster, but his stare continued.

They were sitting alone in the conference room. Blunt had gone to Ramrod Robotics to talk to June about the fate of C3—she just might know what happened. Barry was hovering over the station somewhere, making calls to see if he could locate C3 or Crab Claw Real Estate. Everyone else was in the squad room, working other elements of the case.

She cleared her throat. "Grave?"

He glanced at her, then returned to his faraway stare.

She leaned closer. "Grave, what is it? What are you doing?"

He chewed faster, then swallowed the last remaining bits of a donut. "Thinking."

"And?"

"Have you ever heard the names Brad Dingle or Sloe Jim Phizz?"

She shrugged. "Nope."

"Dingle was the financial guy at C3, and Phizz was its chief designer. They were both madly in love with Wanda. Not that she was in love. She was—*is*—a master manipulator."

"I can see it. She's beautiful, and I learned enough about her on our flight here to know she's disingenuous as all get out."

"I'm thinking we need to find both of them, especially Phizz. He was at work on a neural node the last time I saw him."

Salamander sat up straight. "Really? Those were the precursors to the portal device, or at least part of it. Without the invention of the nodes, the portal would never have been possible."

"Okay," said Grave. "Let's get to work on this. Where's Barry?"

"Making calls, about C3."

"Oh, right."

"Shall we wait for Sergeant Blunt?"

"No, he'll join us eventually."

"So where do we go first?"

Grave looked surprised. "Oh, I see what you mean. No, we don't need to go anywhere. We'll just search their names on the Universal Database. It pretty much knows everything about everyone."

"Wow, we have nothing like that on Mars."

"So you can add the Universal Database to your crater list, and just check it off."

She beamed at him. She was beginning to like this strange old man. A tad.

44

Even God was shaking his head at the results from the search for the portal device. He had taken data and images from the EverEye Satellite, CCTV cameras, GPS Central, and sonar to create a data set that only included land, air, and sea targets from the locations of the three victims and Wanda Orville at the times and locations of their run-in with the portal.

Captain Morgan groaned, or it may have been a heavy sigh, or it may have been a heavy sigh mixed with a groan—a *grigh* or a *sroan* or some such—but it had a sound loud enough to reach everyone in the room. "Are you sure, God?"

God slumped back in his seat. "I've run the data five times now, and I still get the same results: three hoverbuses, six hovercars, three hovercycles, five big hovertrucks, and a hoverscooter on land; four sailing boats, two light freighters, six tankers, fourteen speedboats, and two submarines on or under water; and two private planes, four freighter drones, a Navy cargo plane, two passenger liners, thirty-seven drones, and a single passenger dirigible by air.

Grave had an idea. "Can we refine the data, maybe focus on what shows up within, say, twenty yards of the portal device?"

God nodded. "We can, but it will take all night."

"Let's do that," said Morgan. He looked at the tired faces of his team. "I know we've been at it a while, but let me ask a couple of questions before we call it a day. God will have fresh data for us tomorrow morning, and I'd rather have fresh minds and faces review it all." He yawned. "Including myself. Now, Grave, where do we stand with the search for C3?"

"It seems to have vanished from the earth. No forwarding address, no filing of papers to dissolve the company, no recent tax records. They're just gone."

"And the staff?"

"Nothing, at least on Earth." He nodded at Salamander. "But Salamander is checking on the possibility that they may be on Mars."

Salamander nodded. "Yes, I'm hoping to have more information in the morning. There's no one by those names on Mars, but thanks to Grave, I've provided them with photos of them. A search is underway."

"Are you sure it was C3 involved in the device's manufacture?"

Salamander nodded. "Yes, I worked in the portal at least once a week, tracking down suspects. The name C3 was all over it. The same logo that's on their abandoned building."

Morgan grighed. "Okay, let's call it a day."

Everyone pushed back their chairs and began to work their way out of the room. As Grave passed by Morgan, Morgan grabbed him by the arm. "Not you. I need a word."

"Okay," said Grave. He turned to Salamander, who was almost out the door. "Could you wait for me? It will just be a minute."

She nodded and left the room.

Morgan grighed again.

"What is it, sir?"

Morgan whispered, "I'm just wondering how Salamander is working out."

Grave wasn't sure what he was getting at. "She's been fine, a little gruff at times, but she has a fine mind and a keen sense of what needs to be done. Why?"

Morgan shook his head. "Nothing. Just wondering. Okay, out of here. See you in the morning."

Grave nodded and left the room.

Morgan sat back down at the head of the conference table and drummed his fingers. *I really need to retire*, he thought. The next sound out of his month was no sigh, no grigh, but a definite resonant grunt. *I really, really do.*

45

Salamander squirmed in her seat. She had been squirming and smiling politely for what seemed an eternity. She didn't know why Grave and Loblolly had invited her to dinner at Le Crabbe Bleu, but she was uncomfortable being with them. They were clearly in love. You could tell that just by the way they glanced at each other. Or lightly touched each other. Or giggled. Never in her life had she been exposed to such icky behavior. Worse, Loblolly was making a point of looking directly at her whenever she touched Grave's arm or cooed at him.

"I think I should be going," she said.

She started to stand, but Grave motioned her back in her seat. "No, no, our food will be here soon."

"I'm not that hungry, and I have things to do."

"Nonsense. We'll have a fine meal, and then talk more about the case."

She sighed. "As you wish, but are they always this slow?"

Loblolly laughed. "Sometimes even slower, but the food—oh, my god, you just wait and see."

They waited. Salamander squirmed. Grave and Loblolly giggled. And cooed. And touched.

And then Grave pointed at Salamander's salamander tattoo. "I know that was an award, an honor, but what's the backstory?"

Salamander stopped squirming and looked at each of them in turn. "Yes, an honor, but much more. As you know, Mars was once teeming with life, but most of it has no fossil record. In fact, the only fossil we've found on Mars is a red salamander, and it's much like the salamanders you have here on Earth."

"Interesting," said Grave, "but I still don't understand why you'd choose that as a symbol of honor."

"Well, the explanation is a bit slithery, just like a salamander. The thing is, life is fragile, right. And if you ask any ecologist here on Earth how to evaluate the health of an ecosystem, most of them will point you to the most fragile species. In many case, particularly here on your east coast, they'd choose the salamander as their exemplar of health."

"So, your actions contributed to the health of your ecosystem, of Mars," said Loblolly. "And thus the tattoo."

"Exactly," said Salamander. "Yes, my first, but certainly not my last."

Loblolly laughed. "Oh, and what will be your next tattoo?"

"I'm thinking a crab tattoo."

They both laughed at her.

"No, seriously, it will serve as a reminder not to chase red herrings. I'm sure you've both figured out that the crab tattoos have nothing to do with anything."

Grave blinked. "They don't?"

"Of course not," said Salamander.

"I don't get it, either," said Loblolly.

"Come on," said Salamander. "Is there anything mysterious or nefarious about the crab tattoo you share with Snoot?"

Loblolly shook her head. "No, no, those were just a friend thing, a partner thing."

"Exactly," said Salamander. "Now, you may not believe me now, Grave, but in the end, you'll have to."

Grave started to respond, but Loblolly grabbed his arm. "Save it for later, the food is finally here."

And come it did, held high on a tray by a young man dressed all in white and followed by two assistants, who whisked the plates of food off the tray and placed them in front of the cooing, squirming party of three. And with a final flourish, the servers dumped a dozen steaming crabs in the center of the table, presenting each of the party with their own little wooden mallet. And with that, they left as quickly as they had arrived.

Salamander was bug-eyed. "Crabs? Really?"

"The absolute best," said Loblolly, placing one in front of herself and slamming her mallet down on it, seasoning and shell fragments spraying across the table.

Grave raised his eyebrows and chuckled. "She's still learning."

"I can see that," said Salamander. "I can see that."

She picked up a crab, carefully removed all its claws and legs, except for the back fins on either side. Then with her fingers, she pried the apron off, stuck her thumb in the resulting hole, and pulled the shell off, revealing the crab's lungs.

Grave gawped at her. "You've had crabs already?"

She shook her head. "No, I just watched an inflight video." She looked down at the open crab. "Yuck. Are you sure this is edible?"

"Well, not the lungs and such. Pull those off."

"Right." She pulled off the lungs and other internal organs right down to the fat. "You call this mustard, right?"

"Yes, and you can eat that."

She picked up the crab, broke it in half, and gave one of the halves a quick twist, revealing succulent meat, which she pulled off and held high. "Here we go."

She popped the little piece of crab into her mouth, her eyes growing wide. "Oh, my."

For the next hour, her every move was a master class in the disassembly and consumption of steamed, Old Bay seasoned, Maryland blue crabs. By the end of that hour, even Loblolly was getting the hang of it.

"Should we order more?" said Salamander. "I could eat these all night."

Grave chuckled. "I have a better idea."

"Like what?"

Grave looked toward a waiter approaching the table. "Dessert. A very special dessert."

The waiter set down a large chocolate cake. "Enjoy," he said, before disappearing in a way reminiscent of a waiter disappearing just when you're looking for him.

Salamander looked down at it. "It's just a cake."

"Oh, no," said Grave. "This is a Smith Island Cake. Here, I'll show you why it's so special." He picked up a knife, cut out a wedge, and placed it on a small plate in front of Salamander.

She blinked. "So many layers."

"Exactly," said Loblolly. She leaned in toward the cake. "This one has eight layers, but some can go as many as fifteen layers."

Salamander shook her head. "Why would anyone go to so much trouble making those layers?"

"Good question," said Grave. "As you've already guessed, this cake originated on Smith Island, home to watermen and their families who worked the bay for oysters. Wives there would give their husbands one of these when the watermen left the island to harvest oysters. The layers, and the difficulty of making them, were meant to remind the men of the community they had left behind."

"More than that," said Loblolly. "The cakes were a way of blessing the harvest and telling the watermen that they were loved and would be missed."

"Wow," said Salamander. "I'd like to see this island. Can we go there sometime, Simon?"

He shook his head. "No, Smith Island was a low, flat island, and it fell beneath the waters in 2050, along with most islands in the Bay."

"So sad," said Salamander. She picked up a fork and took a bite of the cake. "Wonderful, just wonderful." She looked down at the cake, then turned to Grave. "Thank you both for this evening. It has been wonderful."

Loblolly reached over and put her hand on Salamander's arm. "Just a way of saying welcome."

Salamander's eyes glistened. "Stop, you guys, you're making me all teary and shit." She brushed away her tears. "So, Simon, you said you wanted to talk about the case?"

He shook his head. "It's getting late. We can wait until tomorrow."

"No, I had a couple of ideas."

"Oh?"

"Yes. If those men you mentioned—Dingle and Phizz—are on Mars, they would have had to get there by way of the Mars Terminal. We could check the passenger lists going back to the day Orville fled."

"That's a great idea," said Simon.

Salamander smiled. "And we could do the same thing for people arriving at the Mars Terminal. Perhaps they're back here and not on Mars."

"Makes sense," said Loblolly.

Grave nodded. "I had another thought, about that portal device. How long would it take to build one?"

"I'm not sure," said Salamander. "I guess the biggest job would be making the cylinder itself. The rest are parts easily acquired from various sources here in Crab Cove."

"So we should be looking for a large warehouse or manufacturing plant," said Grave.

"Or someplace like the abandoned C3 building," said Salamander. "That would be plenty big enough."

"We need to get in there," said Grave. He looked at his watch. "Who's game for an adventure?"

46

The angles and demon geometry of the C3 building were even stranger at night, moonlight making the building glow with an eerie blue light. Grave had left his Sprite back at Le Crabbe Bleu to keep their arrival as secret as possible. He and Salamander had climbed into Loblolly's take-home police hovercruiser and held their breath as Loblolly's lead foot took them through the city center in record time. She slowed only when they entered the parking lot, where she had killed her headlights and coasted into a parking spot.

"What now?" said Salamander. "How do we get in without breaking glass?"

"No problem," said Loblolly. "Laser gun. Cuts through anything."

"Wow."

"Indeed. We've had them for only a few months, but they're really cool. You can dial up the material you want to cut through, and the laser adjusts."

"Can I take one of those babies back to Mars? We don't have anything like that, and we should."

"I'll talk to Morgan," said Grave. "I don't see why not."

Loblolly climbed out of the car. "Come on, let's get this done."

Grave and Salamander followed her to the back of the hovercruiser and watched as she popped the trunk and pulled out a gun that looked like Grave's childhood dream of a pew-pew-pew ray gun, one that would dispatch aliens with ease.

"Impressive," said Salamander. "Now, let's see it work."

They walked up the steps to the entrance.

"Stand back," said Loblolly, raising the gun.

A laser shot out from it, alternating colors from green to red to blue to some color resembling rust as it carved a man-sized hole in the glass door, the glass finally falling into the building and shattering on the floor.

"Jeez," said Grave. "I didn't think it would make that much noise."

Loblolly shrugged. "Oh, well. Come on, let's go in."

They squeezed through the hole and crunched through the glass in the lobby, each pulling out a flashlight to make their way deeper into the building.

Grave pointed down a hallway. "As I recall, Phizz's lab is down this way. It would be big enough to hold a few of those devices."

They followed Grave down the hall, then something unexpected happened.

Flashlights! Coming in their direction!

Before they had a chance to run or draw weapons, the lights were in their faces. A voice boomed at them. "Stop!"

It was a familiar voice, one they had all heard earlier in the day. Grave shielded his eyes with a hand. "Captain Morgan?"

"Yes, of course it's me. What in hell are you guys doing here?"

"Looking for the device," said Loblolly.

"What was that noise?" said Morgan.

"Um," said Loblolly. "We had to get in, so . . ."

"You used the new laser," said Morgan. "Holy Christ, how are we going to explain that?"

"Wait," said Grave. "How did you get in?"

Morgan sighed. "Keys, Grave, *keys.*"

"So you have a warrant?"

"Of course not. Judge Mallow would never countenance this."

"So now we have a double break-in," said Salamander. She shook her head. "Wow."

Two other lights approached.

"Indeed," said God.

"Exactly," said Snoot.

Grave snorted. "Jeez, how many people are here?"

"Just the three of us," said Morgan.

"Did you find anything?" said Grave.

Morgan nodded. "We did. Come on, all of you, you've got to see this."

They all turned and walked down to Phizz's darkened lab. At first they saw nothing, just lab equipment and the usual electronic meters and measuring devices. But then Morgan shined a light on five tall cylinders.

Grave gasped. "Portals!"

47

Salamander moved from cylinder to cylinder, her mouth agape as she went from one to the next, each a different size, the smallest seven feet tall and three feet in diameter, the largest what looked like eight feet in diameter and fifteen feet high, it's top edge almost scraping the ceiling.

She took a few steps back and held up her arms. "This isn't possible. Look at that one, it's huge."

Morgan walked down the line of cylinders, rapping his knuckles on each one, the sound growing deeper as he went from the smallest to the largest. "But here they are. The question, or at least one question, is are they operational?"

"And who made them?" said God.

"And why?" said Snoot.

"And why different sizes?" said Loblolly

"And for what purpose, or purposes?" said Grave.

Salamander knew it was her turn to pose a question, and she was not shy about it. "And why is one missing?"

Everyone turned to her and almost as one said, "What?"

"See here, on the floor, a circular impression on the floor. Four feet in diameter by my estimation."

"So someone's out there with one," said Morgan. "The same one that killed those women, do you think?"

"Maybe," said Salamander. "Probably."

Morgan turned to the other cylinders. "Salamander, can you tell if these are operational?"

"Yes, of course."

She started walking toward one of the smaller ones, but a bright greenish-blue flash made her stop and turn back toward the impression in the floor, which was now filled with a glowing, steaming cylinder. "What the—"

There was a click, and then a door in the cylinder slid open. A woman in a Martian pressure suit stepped out and looked around. "What the—"

She fumbled with some latches on her helmet and tugged it off. Everyone except Salamander took a step back and stared in disbelief.

Morgan was the first to speak. "Tilda?"

48

Retective Tilda Must looked around at the surprised familiar faces and the face of a strange woman in a red pantsuit and decided that something had gone wrong. "This isn't Mars, is it?"

Morgan shook his head and then shook it again, words finally coming. "No, it's not."

"Crab Cove?"

"Yes."

"On Earth?"

"Indeed."

She puffed out a deep breath. "Wow." She looked back at the cylinder, which was still steaming. "I just stepped into that thing and cleared my throat. The door shut, then immediately opened, and now I'm here, 235 million miles from the mine I was supposed to be in."

"Mine?" said Salamander. "Why a mine?"

"Tracking down a missing person."

"Who?"

"A young woman named Phoebe Denalia, a Martian research scientist. Missing for a couple of days, and apparently in possession of Martian Colony secrets."

"What kind of secrets?" said Morgan.

"I'm not at liberty to say."

"What do you mean, you work for us."

"Not while I'm a member of the Mars Security Force, sir. There are rules at play here, and you know my feelings about rules."

Morgan sighed. He did, but he had to press her on the point. "Well, now that you're *back* on Earth, those rules no longer apply."

"Wait," said Salamander. "You don't want to do that."

Morgan rolled his eyes. "And why not?"

"We're going to need her to be our eyes and ears on Mars."

"What, send her back?"

"Yes, she obviously stepped into the wrong cylinder. Right, Tilda?"

She shrugged. "There was another cylinder there, so yeah, I guess."

"Okay," said Salamander. "Firstly, Ms. Denalia is dead, a victim of whoever created these advanced cylinders."

"Oh."

"Exactly, but even so, we want you to go through the motions trying to find her on Mars. As you do, we want you to look for anyone seemingly in charge of these cylinders."

Morgan interrupted. "And we're looking for two people in particular, Brad Dingle and Sloe Jim Phizz, former employees at this facility here."

"What do they look like?"

"Don't worry," said Morgan. "We'll get you pics of each of them."

Salamander turned to Loblolly. "Do you have the pics?"

Loblolly nodded, reached into her pocket, and pulled out the folded pics. "Here you go."

Salamander took the pics and shoved them into Tilda's hands. "Now put your helmet back on, go back to Mars, and find these guys."

"And keep us up to speed on whatever you find or don't find," said Morgan.

Tilda nodded, put on her helmet, and walked back into the cylinder. The door started to close, and Salamander suddenly stuck her hand out and stopped the door. "Wait, wait, wait, I need to go, too."

"Why?" said Morgan, taken aback. "We need you here."

"I want to talk to Orville's cellmate. We need to know whether Wanda is a victim or part of these murders."

"But you don't have a helmet," said Grave.

"Don't need one. Tilda only needs one because she's heading for the mine."

Tilda stuck her helmeted head out of the door. "Wait, I still need to do that?"

"Yes," said Salamander. "You need to pretend you didn't take the wrong portal device. Go to the mine, do what you were supposed to do."

"Look for a missing person who's dead?"

"Exactly."

Tilda nodded and pulled her head back into the cylinder.

Salamander turned to Morgan. "I'll keep in touch, call you on space comms."

Morgan was still not convinced of the wisdom of what she was planning. "Aren't you worried your superiors will find out you're back?"

"No, I won't be anywhere near them. I'll go from the cylinder to a shuttle and head for Phobos, the penal colony. No one there will suspect anything."

Morgan scratched his head. "All right . . . I guess."

Salamander leaped into the cylinder, the door closed, and the cylinder disappeared in a greenish-blue flash.

Morgan looked around at his still-stunned detectives. "Okay, guys, we need to consider this place a crime scene. Get the Larrys and give Polk a call. We need them here, stat."

49

The penal colony was nothing more than a large cave that had been modified to hold 200 prisoners at maximum capacity. There was only one way in and one way out, through a heavily armored door as tall as two men. On the other side of the door was a small anteroom for visitors and a shuttle docking area that could accommodate six shuttles.

Salamander only had to say her name to gain access to the docking ports. A smile and a wave of her hand was enough to get her past the guard, who knew her well.

Peter Bland was a small man, and round, and like Captain Morgan, seemed to be wearing a uniform one size too small.

He seemed to be amused at the sight of her. "Back already?"

She chuckled. "They send me when they send me, right?"

He laughed. "They do, they do." He held out his hand. "Papers?"

Salamander reached into her pocket and then feigned surprise. "Oh, shit, I must have left them behind."

"Salamander, that's so not like you." He looked back at the shuttle doors. "Maybe in the shuttle?"

She shook her head and pretended to be crestfallen. "Oh, man, Peter, I've got to get in. They'll screw me over if I don't conduct this interview."

"Who you seeing?"

She rolled her eyes and slapped her arms against her sides. "The name is on the papers."

"So you have no idea who you want to see. I can't just let you in to wander around, you know."

"Remember that Orville bitch?"

He rolled his eyes. "Oh do I. Beautiful but a real piece of work."

"Well, it's her cellmate I need to see. Get her testimony for Orville's trial."

He shook his head. "Sorry, girl, no papers, no entrance."

Salamander gave him her best woe-is-little-old-me wheedling look. "Come on, Peter, you know me."

He crossed his arms across his substantive stomach. "Go to lunch with me."

"Lunch?"

"Yes, you want in, I want lunch—with you, *today*."

Salamander let out a deep breath, frowned at him, and then said, "Deal!"

50

Polk and his team had been examining the cylinders and Phizz's laboratory for over an hour, much to the frustration of Captain Morgan, who wanted results, answers—*now.*

"Jeremy, are you done yet?"

Polk rolled his eyes. "You want the examination to be over before it has barely begun. Every time, Henry, *every single time.*"

"I need to know."

"Know, shmoe. You're just like me. In a job too long and impatient to go."

Morgan shook his head. "Tried retirement once, didn't like it."

"Well, maybe you should give it a shot again. Me, too."

"You can't be serious, Jeremy. You, retire? The world would wrench from its axis and roll away."

Polk sighed. "Okay, enough of this." He paused, trying to calm himself. "This is what we've found so far." He pointed at a lab bench, where a tennis ball and a small plant were sitting.

Morgan blinked. "A tennis ball? And a weed? That's it?"

"No, of course not, Henry. But look at all these surfaces. Prints take time and care and patience."

Morgan had been through this many times with Polk. "How long?"

"We've taken as many prints as we could. We'll send them to the print people for identification, so you won't know anything on those until later today, perhaps even as late as tomorrow."

"Damn, why does everything take so long?"

"It doesn't, Henry. At least where DNA is concerned. At least not anymore."

"What are you talking about?"

"I received some new equipment last month. State-of-the-art stuff. I simply have to scan the room and the device identifies the person and the location of the DNA."

"Wow, so let's get to it. Scan the room."

"Already done, Henry, and I think the results will make you happy—and confused."

"What did you find?"

"A lot of people, Henry. No, a *ton* of people, some familiar, some obscure, and some surprising as all get out."

"Come on, then, what did you find?"

Polk patted his pockets, eventually finding a list and holding it up to his eyes. "Let's see here. First off, we found people you'd expect to find. Phizz, all the Orvilles, and Dingle, as well as you, Freeman, Snoot, Loblolly, Salamander, and of course, Grave and Blunt."

"Who else?"

"Okay, here's where it gets interesting, Henry. You ready?"

Morgan sighed. "Of course I'm ready. Who, dammit?"

Polk cleared his throat and continued. "Heather Van Hinkle, Koos Van Hinkle, Larry Flan, Jacky Pompo, Manley Morris, Sally Fifth, Judy Dupree, Viv Val, and Phoebe Denalia."

Morgan had reached the point of disbelief at the second name and just grew more and more amazed as each name was read. "You can't be serious."

"Oh, but I am. This new tool doesn't lie."

Morgan looked down at the tennis ball and the plant. "And where did you find those?"

"In the big cylinder. And all the people were in there, too, at one time or another."

"Together, you think, at the same time?"

Polk shrugged. "Maybe."

Morgan reached down into his fulsome repertoire of expressions and let loose. "Great oogly-boogly."

51

Salamander sat on the bed opposite Melanie Mude, Orville's former cellmate, and tried to get through the barrier of controlling drugs served up by the guards morning, noon, and night. She leaned forward and snapped her fingers in front of Mude's face. The girl, who couldn't have been more than fifteen, lifted her head briefly, but it was clear she was unable to focus on Salamander. She was as diminutive as Jeremy Polk, her legs dangling over the edge of the bed, her feet not touching the floor. Her dark-rimmed eyes, gray and cloudy, seemed to be staring at a spot somewhere behind Salamander. In fact, everything about her was dark, the only color coming from her red-striped prison garb.

"Um," she said. Her voice was high-pitched, more like a toddler than a teenager.

"Good, good," said Salamander. "Focus on me."

The girl blinked, then scratched her shaved head, which was covered with scars and scabs from previous scratches, a few blond hairs peeking through. "Um?"

"I'm Detective Kismet Salamander of the Mars Security Force, and I have a few questions for you about your former cellmate, Wanda Orville."

The name seemed to bring her out of the fog. "Who?"

"Orville. Wanda Orville. Do you remember her?"

Mude looked left and right and then dropped to the floor and scurried under the bed.

Salamander tried to grab her by the arm and tug her out, but the girl retreated to the wall, flattening her body against it. "Melanie, come out from there."

Mude shook her head and looked away. "No."

"I need to talk to you about Wanda Orville."

The name seemed to strike her like a heavy blow from an ax. She curled up into a ball and whimpered, "Bitch."

52

Morgan was the last one in the C3 boardroom, a room that like the rest of the building, featured strange angles and glass. The boardroom table was glass, the walls were glass, the floor was glass, the ceiling was glass—even the chairs were glass. When you sat in those chairs, you had the dizzying feeling that you were suspended in space, with no solid ground in sight.

Morgan shook his head. "Look at this place. It's like sitting inside a diamond or something." He pulled out a chair and sat down. "Anyway, let's get to it. You've seen the list of people who've been in those cylinders. We've interviewed every last one of them, and they've apparently lied to us."

"We should bring them in," said God. "Show them our wrath."

Morgan chuckled. "God's wrath, eh? Well, maybe."

"I agree with God," said Grave, "though not necessarily the wrath part—at least not yet."

Charlize raised a hand. "I've interviewed them, and they're all lying about something. There's more than murders here. A conspiracy of some kind, I should think."

"I had the same feeling," said Smithers. "They do that thing that all humans seem to do when they're lying."

"Blinking, you mean?" said Grave.

"Yes, exactly."

Loblolly raised her hand. "Obviously, it has something to do with the cylinders. Maybe it's some sort of business arrangement. You know, you've got these portal devices that can take you millions of miles in the blink of an eye. That's worth something. That's worth a lot."

"The scientific importance of this is incalculable," said Smithers. "It opens the universe to us."

"Which means big bucks for its owner," said Snoot. "Maybe all that DNA in that large cylinder is a result of a demonstration to potential investors? A quick trip to Mars or the Moon to open their wallets."

Morgan nodded. "That's possible."

"It is," said Grave, "but these people on the list don't strike me as high rollers. All that connects them is the country club and a tennis tournament."

Charlize nodded. "It's strange, all right, and I agree that we should bring them all in. We'll need to keep them separated, so they can't speak to one another."

"Exactly," said Morgan, "so unless someone has a better idea, I'd say let's get out there, bring them into the station, and find out what the hell is going on."

Everyone nodded except Charlize. "Before we do that, I'd like to talk about the victims a minute."

Morgan sat back in his chair and waved his hand. "The floor is yours." He looked down. "If you can find it."

"Up until now, sir, we've assumed at least two of the victims were collateral damage, innocents who saw something they shouldn't have and were killed for it."

"Yes," said Morgan. "So?"

"This new DNA evidence suggests that both victims knew about the cylinders, were in the cylinders."

"So you think they were somehow part of this, um, whatever is going on?"

"Yes. I think that they were in the process of escaping from something, perhaps even with the third victim, Phoebe Denalia."

"So we're back to a conspiracy of some kind," said Snoot. "And maybe the victims no longer wanted to be a part of it."

"I agree," said Grave. "Unless you believe in coincidences—and I don't—you have to come to that conclusion. They were involved somehow and wanted out."

Morgan held up his hands. "Hold on, let's not go down that road—or any road—until Polk has finished his work and we've had a chance to interview the suspects."

Grave was about to agree, but out of the corner of his eye he saw someone in a Mars pressure suit, complete with helmet, walking quickly down the hall toward the boardroom.

"What's this?" said Grave, pointing at the hallway.

Everyone turned to see the figure pushing into the room.

"It's me," said Salamander, tugging off her helmet. "You ready for some crazy shit."

53

Everyone in the boardroom was more than eager to hear what Salamander had learned on Mars, but Salamander herself was more determined to take off her pressure suit, holding up a hand to stop their entreaties to begin until she had tugged off the suit and kicked it into a corner of the boardroom. "That thing's hot."

Everyone looked at her.

She looked at them. "Oh, oh right. Let me just find a seat."

She moved around the table to an empty chair next to Snoot. "Okay, I was able to gain access to Orville's cellmate, a 15-year-old girl named Melanie Mude, currently serving a life sentence for murdering her parents."

"Wow," said Grave.

Salamander shrugged. "Pretty common on Mars, really. Our parents chose to go to Mars, we didn't, and the contrast between life on Mars and life on Earth is striking. Earth is like an ice cream sundae to us. We all want to be here, not there, so sometimes tensions reach the breaking point."

She looked around the table. Everyone was nodding. "Okay, so she was reluctant to say anything at first, but then I got her to talk. She said that Wanda Orville went on and on about how she was going to escape prison on Earth, that she was sure that her lover Sloe Jim Phizz would rescue her. When Melanie had scoffed at that, Orville had said, and I quote, 'Think what you want, but when Jim comes for me, no one will be able to find us—*ever*.'"

Morgan raised a finger. "A question. Did Orville ever have visitors?"

"Good question, sir, and I asked it, but her answer was no."

"So where is Jim Phizz?"

"Not on Mars," said Salamander, "or at least that's what Retective Must says. Her search came up empty. She even checked passenger logs, coming and going, and there was no Sloe Jim Phizz."

"He could have come under another name," said Grave.

"Of course," said Salamander, "but if he did come, why not visit his lover?"

"Good point," said Snoot, then raised her eyebrows. "Wait, did Orville have access to comms?"

Salamander nodded. "She did, and thank you, I forgot to mention that. In the months she was interred there, she received ten calls, seven from Earth, and three—the most recent—from the Hilton hotel orbiting Mars."

"Wow," said Charlize. "So maybe he was there, at the hotel."

"It's possible," said Salamander. "Even probable. I mean, who else would be in contact with her? Not Brad Dingle. He's in prison here on Earth."

"True," said Grave, "but Dingle could have called her from prison. You know, one of the calls from Earth."

"There should be a record of that," said Morgan, turning to God. "See what you can find."

God nodded. "I'll check on all ten calls, sir. Perhaps this Dingle person is involved. I mean, if the portal can snatch Orville out of our jail, why not Dingle from prison?"

Morgan slumped back in his chair. "We're making progress. Slow progress, but progress nonetheless." He turned to Salamander. "Before you arrived, we were talking about bringing all the suspects into the station to be interviewed. We need to press them harder. Some or all of them have been lying."

Salamander shook her head. "Not the station, sir. Here, at C3. Anyone who knows what's going on is going to be very nervous that we know at least part of what's going on, too."

"I think that's a great idea," said Grave. "And there's plenty of room here to isolate them from one another. Plenty of offices and conference rooms."

Everyone nodded.

"Okay," said Morgan. "We want to be careful about how we do this. Try to make each person think our focus is on them alone."

God raised his hand. "If I might make a suggestion . . ."

"Of course," said Morgan. "What did you have in mind?"

"Let me and the other Larrys handle this. Our arrival on their doorstep won't alarm them as much as you showing up."

"That's a great idea," said Loblolly. "You just tell them we have a few more questions."

"That we want their *perspective* on things," said Snoot.

Morgan chuckled. "I love it."

"And while we're making suggestions," said Salamander, "I'd like to suggest that we not rush into this, that we take the time to do background checks on each of the suspects and each of the victims. We know very little about any of them. Who are they? How do they know each other, and so on."

Morgan frowned. "That will take a day, maybe more."

"It will be worth it, sir. With that information we stand a better chance of manipulating them than the other way around."

"She makes a good point," said Grave.

Morgan puffed out his cheeks. "I don't know, I worry about those cylinders and the killer suddenly disappearing."

"I can help with the cylinders, sir," said Salamander.

"Oh?"

"They've been enhanced, but their basic operation is the same. I can turn them on and off, and most important, lock them down."

Morgan smiled. "Excellent. Okay, let's take twenty-four hours to do background checks." He turned to God. "And you can double-check on those calls, as well as the passenger lists and any CCTV footage at the Mars Terminal for departing and arriving travelers."

"That's a lot," said God.

"Well, you're God, aren't you?"

God shook his head and smiled at Morgan. "Good one, sir."

"I thought you'd like that," said Morgan. He turned to the others. "Now, before we go, let's at least decide who's interviewing who, in which office, and when. The order of these interviews could be critical."

"All the more reason to conduct the background checks," said Salamander.

Morgan frowned at her. "You've already made your point, Salamander." There was a tone of scolding in his voice, and the tone was not lost on Salamander.

"Yes, sir," she said, looking down at the table.

Morgan turned away from her and took a deep breath. "Now, who wants to interview Koos Van Hinkle?"

As the hands shot up, God interrupted. "Sir, if I'm to complete my tasks in a timely manner, I'm afraid I must get started on it right away."

"Okay," said Morgan, "go."

God nodded, pushed back his chair, and gave everyone a little godly wave. "Miracles don't happen overnight, but in this case, they will."

"Good," said Morgan. "We could use a few miracles right about now." He turned to the others. "Now, let's see those hands again. Who wants Koos?"

The hands shot up, a choice was made, another name was named, the hands shot up, and choice after choice was made.

54

After the meeting broke up, Grave followed Salamander down the hall that led to Phizz's lab, where the cylinders were stored. "Mind if I tag along? I'd like to learn more about those cylinders."

She shrugged. "Sure, no problem."

They walked quietly down the hall and into the lab. The cylinders sat there doing nothing.

"I'll just be a minute," said Salamander, walking into one of the smallest cylinders.

"What are you doing?"

She poked her head back out of the cylinder door. "Making sure they stay put. The last thing we need is someone taking one or retrieving one or all of them to some unknown location."

"Oh, good thinking."

As Salamander moved from cylinder to cylinder, Grave moved around the lab, taking note of the tennis ball and the plant sitting on one of the lab benches. He remembered encountering Sloe Jim and Wanda here, the two of them locked in an embrace behind a piece of equipment. He looked around the lab. Whatever that piece of equipment was, it was long gone.

He walked across the lab to Phizz's small office, which was just big enough to accommodate a small desk and a chair. He picked up a paper from the top of the desk, one of many scattered there.

The Key Elements of Travel through Interstellar Space, by Drs. S. J. Phizz and P. Denalia

It was just the title page, nothing more. He looked through the other papers on the desk, but there was nothing that remotely suggested a treatise on space travel. He took the title page and walked back into the lab. Salamander was just emerging from the last, and largest, cylinder.

"Okay," she said. "We're good to go."

"Great," said Grave, looking at this watch. "How about an early dinner?"

She shook her head. "Dinner, yes, but first I'd like to talk to your Miss Victoria again. I have some questions for her and the late Phoebe Denalia."

"Speaking of whom, take a look at this." He handed her the title page.

She smiled up at him. "Not surprised, and I think we'll learn more when God finishes his background research. To me, the murders seem to be a plan gone wrong."

"Or a plan gone right."

"What? You think the murders were part of the plan?"

"Not necessarily. I just like to keep alternatives in mind. Not dismissing them out of hand. I've found out the hard way that if you charge along in one direction, you lose sight of the other directions."

She squinted at him in an appraising way. "Detective Grave, you are full of surprises."

Grave chuckled. "I try."

"Come on, then, let's head for the cemetery."

"In my Sprite?"

She rolled her eyes. "Never, *ever*. I'm surprised you have any hearing left."

"It helps me think."

"Whatever. I'll take my hovercyle and meet you there. Try to keep up."

And with that, she ran from the lab, down the hall, and out into the parking lot. By the time Grave raced from the building, she was already speeding away.

Grave knew there was no way the little Sprite could keep up with a hovercycle, so he just strolled to the Sprite, started it up, and drove slowly out of the parking lot, the gospel music growing louder and louder.

55

The passenger lists and flight check-in photographs turned out to be God's easiest task. There was no sign of Sloe Jim Phizz on the outbound flights to Mars, but halfway through the return flight photos, the computer kicked out a single image that left no doubt: Sloe Jim had been on Mars and had returned to Earth under an assumed name a month ago.

But where had he been all this time, and where was he now?

It was a perplexing problem, even for God, so he turned to the next task at hand: background checks on Heather Van Hinkle, Koos Van Hinkle, Larry Flan, Jacky Pompo, Manley Morris, Sally Fifth, Judy Dupree, Viv Val, and Phoebe Denalia.

God set the parameters for the search, directing the computer to search bank records, employment records, school records, police records, and phone records, both those from the now displaced cellphones and from the suspects' drone phones. He also directed the computer to do cross-checks, looking for links and associations, calls between the suspects, and so on.

The computer buzzed and hummed, then stopped briefly to provide an estimate on the necessary processing time: twenty-two minutes.

God sighed. "Why so long?"

"Sir?"

God turned to see an image of himself, another Larry in a police uniform, one of several scurrying around the squad room. "Nothing, didn't mean to speak out loud."

"The results of the search on the air, land, and sea traffic at the time of the murders is in."

God leaped to his feet. "What?"

"I said—"

"I know what you said, now tell me the results."

The officer handed God a single sheet of paper. "Here, here it is."

God scanned the document. "Ha!"

He looked over at Captain Morgan's empty office. "Where's Morgan? We have to find Morgan."

56

Salamander reached the cemetery first and was already sitting next to Victoria, in deep conversation, before Grave could make it up the hill with Barry.

"Oh, there you are," said Victoria, looking up. "Kismet and I have been having a fine conversation about death. Did you know that on Mars they *dissolve* the body? I just can't imagine it."

Grave took a deep breath—that hill seemed to be getting steeper and steeper—and sat down next to Victoria. "I did, and yes, it's strange."

"Not if you were on Mars," said Salamander.

Grave looked up at Barry. "You can tour the cemetery if you like."

Barry wobbled in the air. "Yes, sir, and might I add it's nice to see you talking to an actual person on this bench."

"You may, and now you may go."

Barry lifted high into the air and was gone.

"Now," said Grave, "we have some questions for Phoebe Denalia."

"Yes, I know," said Victoria. "Kismet has already made the same request."

"And . . ."

"Don't be upset with me, Simon, but she can talk to Miss Phoebe, but you can't."

"What?"

"Phoebe and the other two know you're a detective, you see, and for the second part, they don't want to talk to a man." She turned to Salamander. "So, Phoebe has agreed to talk with Kismet."

"It'll be fine, Grave," said Salamander. "I know what to ask."

Grave threw up his hands. "All right, no problem, I'll just sit here on the bench."

Victoria leaned over and gave him a hug. "Oh, I'm so happy that you understand, Simon." She nodded at Salamander. "Come with me."

They both stood, gave Grave a little wave, and walked down the hill in the direction of the visitor center.

"We're going to the visitor center?" said Salamander.

"No, just behind it, at the new arrival area. That's where we greet all the new arrivals and explain what happens next for each of them."

"And what exactly is that?"

Victoria said nothing, but grabbed Salamander by the hand and pulled her around the side of the Visitor Center. "Back here."

When they reached the back of the center, Salamander gasped. Scores of dead souls were sitting on row after row of folding chairs. An ethereal voice was calling out numbers. "Number seventy-two, we will see you now at window number six."

"What's this?" said Salamander. "And why are there so many of them?"

Victoria smiled. "Processing. The number is high because we're a regional processing center. We pull in the dead from New New York to the southernmost city in New Florida: Jacksonville."

Salamander looked in every direction. "So, where's Phoebe?"

Victoria pointed. "Over there. I set up four chairs, so you could talk to them in privacy."

Salamander saw the chairs and the spirits of Heather Van Hinkle, Judy Dupree, and Phoebe Denalia. "I can speak to all three?"

"Yes, they all seemed quite amenable to it, so I thought, why not?"

Salamander beamed at her. "Thank you!"

Victoria cocked her head. "Don't thank me yet. They all think they're still alive, so don't expect them to be completely cooperative. I've found that many spirits take their secrets to the grave, so what they reveal may not be the full story."

"I'll take my chances," said Salamander.

"Would you like me to go with you? You know, introduce you?"

Salamander considered it. On the one hand, having Victoria introduce her might give Salamander some credibility with the women. On the other hand, maybe not. "No thanks, I'll take it from here."

"As you wish, but just in case you need me, I'll be at Window Five."

Salamander nodded. "Okay, thanks."

She started walking toward the three spirits, who squirmed in their seats at her approach.

Salamander stopped a few steps in front of them. "Hi, I'm Kismet Salamander. I'm new here. Could you help me out?"

57

Captain Morgan knew that he should have stayed at the station and waited it out until news of some kind broke or shattered or exploded into his life, but he was bone tired and needed time away from all the Officer Larrys scurrying around the squad room. So he and Rum had quietly exited the back door and walked the half mile to Morgan's houseboat.

It was just as he had left it, a total mess. Pizza boxes, some containing half-eaten slices of pepperoni pizza, were stacked on the kitchen table and around the living room, along with empty cans of Coke Super. A cloud of fruit flies hovered over the overfull sink.

Morgan took a pizza box off his recliner and plopped down, the chair molding to his body, causing a sigh to erupt from him. "Rum, Rum, Rum, how long can I keep this up?"

"Too long," said Rum, hovering in front of him. "Your vital signs are not what they used to be, even just a few months ago. You need to work on succession and get the hell out of there. You promised me you would retire last year, but no, you had to take on the next case, and the next case, and the next."

"They just keep coming."

Rum wobbled in the air. "That doesn't mean you have to take them."

"But—"

"No buts, captain. If you keep up your current pace, I'm afraid I will have to report you to the medical authorities."

Morgan sat up in his seat. "You wouldn't dare."

"Oh, yeah? Try me."

"Maybe I'll just switch you off or trade you in for a newer model—you're not exactly state-of-the-art, you know."

Rum, taken aback, hovered silently.

"Look," said Morgan. "I know what you're saying is in my best interest, and I will retire, I will, but not until this case is over."

"Promise me you'll set a retirement date and choose your successor—soon."

Morgan nodded. "I promise. Now, if you don't mind, I'd like to take a little nap, restore my energy, in silence."

"Not so fast. Who are you thinking will be your successor?"

Morgan shrugged. "The natural selection is Grave, but he was miserable the last time he filled in for me."

"What about Tilda Must? I think she'd run a tight ship."

Morgan chuckled. "And that ship would sink. No, she's too focused on procedures and rules. You have to be a little loosey-goosey at times, and she'd never manage that. Besides, everyone hates her."

"Well, who, then?"

Morgan ran a hand over his bald head. "Well, actually, I've been giving serious thought to promoting—"

"Wait," said Rum. "Incoming call. Uh-huh, uh-huh, you don't say. Wow, okay, I'll tell him." Rum turned to Morgan. "That was God. He thinks he's found the source of the portal the murderer used to kill those women."

Morgan was already on his feet, racing for the door.

58

Having seen their bodies in death, Salamander struggled hard to focus on them in their after-death forms, three bright spirits—*on an adventure*, they said.

"Where do you think you are?" said Salamander.

"We're at the terminal," said Judy Dupree. Salamander marveled at the pitch of her voice, which was more appropriate for a bird.

"Obviously," said Heather Van Hinkle. Salamander marveled at the way her nose wiggled when she spoke.

Phoebe Denalia pointed at Victoria. "See that little girl over there at Window 5? She told us we'd be on our way soon enough." Salamander marveled at her lips, which were full and pouty.

"And where do you think you're going?" said Salamander.

They all laughed as one.

"It's a secret," said Dupree, holding a finger to her lips.

"You have to be on the list," said Van Hinkle.

"Or be part of the plan," said Denalia.

All three giggled conspiratorially.

"Okay, we'll come back to that," said Salamander. "Now, what's the last thing you remember?"

They all looked puzzled.

"About what?" said Van Hinkle.

"Yeah," said Dupree. "What's the topic?"

"Exactly," said Denalia. "I think you'll have to be more specific."

Van Hinkle raised her hand. "Can I say something?"

"Of course," said Salamander.

"I like your look, that whole red pantsuit vibe. You're rockin' it."

Salamander raised an eyebrow. "Um, thank you."

"Wait, wait, wait," said Dupree. "Isn't that pantsuit from that little shop on the boardwalk?"

Salamander nodded.

Dupree turned to Van Hinkle. "I knew it. Don't you remember? It was in the window of the shop when we ran by there the other night."

Van Hinkle looked puzzled at first, but then she smiled. "Yes, yes, I remember that. We were really running fast, weren't we? That pantsuit was just a blur to me. God, I'm surprised you remember that, Judy."

"Why were you running?" said Salamander.

"I can answer that," said Denalia. "I told them to."

Van Hinkle and Dupree seemed stunned.

"Why?" said Van Hinkle.

"Yeah," said Dupree. "Why on earth would you do that?"

Denalia blinked, then shook her head. "I don't remember. Something about the trip, I think."

"That we should get there early?" said Dupree.

"Maybe," said Denalia, looking confused.

"Wait," said Van Hinkle. "That can't be right. We were running in the wrong direction, down toward the town square."

Dupree shook her head. "No, no, I distinctly remember running to the end of the boardwalk, even under it."

Denalia looked dazed. "All I remember is watching the both of you running along the boardwalk, and then there was this flash and everything went black."

Van Hinkle's eyes went wide. "I remember a flash, too. It was green."

"No, blue," said Dupree. "I'm sure of it."

Denalia took a deep breath and turned to Salamander. "Greenish-blue, actually. And the thing about it was I think I've seen that flash before. Many times. I just can't seem to remember where or why or when."

"Me, too," said Dupree.

"And me," said Van Hinkle.

Salamander looked at their confused and alarmed expressions. "Do you think it has something to do with why you're here?"

"The trip, you mean?" said Van Hinkle.

"Why would it have anything to do with our trip?" said Dupree.

Denalia looked around, alarmed. "Wait, this isn't the right terminal." She turned to Salamander. "Where are we, anyway?"

Salamander sighed, then pointed over at Victoria. "That little girl over there will explain everything to you when we're finished talking. Can I ask another question?"

Denalia nodded. "Of course, but where the hell are we?"

Salamander nodded in Victoria's direction. "She'll tell you in a minute. Now, if this isn't the right terminal, what is, and where are you going?"

All three women started to speak, then stopped.

"Come on," said Salamander. "Think."

Van Hinkle looked at the sky. Dupree screwed up her face. And Denalia crossed her arms and closed her eyes.

Van Hinkle was the first to speak. "At the tennis match, the finals. We're to meet center court. Viv Val is going to win it, I just know it. If I had just worked more on my forehand and my serve, I could have won it all."

"Nonsense," said Dupree. "Your forehand and serve are the best in tennis. No, I think it's your backhand. You lost so many points in that last match of yours because of your backhand."

"Really?" said Van Hinkle. "I would have thought—"

"Wait," said Salamander. "Is the court really a terminal?"

"No," said Denalia. "Where we're supposed to meet has a lot of cylinders. There's no cylinders at a tennis court."

Van Hinkle crossed her arms. "I'm sure it's the tennis court. I remember dad insisting on it."

"Yes, now I remember," said Dupree. "At the last meeting, we changed the departure location, but it's not the tennis court."

"Quiet," said Denalia. "That's a secret." She turned to Salamander and gave her a stern look. "I think we're done here."

"But where are we?" said Van Hinkle.

"And why are we here?" said Dupree.

Salamander looked over at Victoria and gave her a little wave. Victoria nodded and began walking toward them.

"Victoria can answer all your questions. Afterwards, I hope you can answer a few more of mine."

"As if," said Denalia, turning away from her.

59

Grave sat alone on Victoria's Victoria-free bench and stared up at the low clouds scudding across the sky out of the northwest. Then he looked over his shoulder, down the hill in the direction Victoria had taken Salamander. Nothing.

He looked at his watch. They had been gone only twenty minutes, but it seemed an eternity to Grave, who had little patience for patience, particularly when it came to murder investigations. Yes, it had only been a couple of days—not long in the scheme of things—but they seemed to be chasing their tails, going hither and yon with every new development.

He looked at his watch again. A minute had passed. *Maybe I should go down the path and see the reverend,* he thought. It had been months since he'd stopped at the Reverend Bendigo Bottoms' gravesite. Bottoms, even dead, was a trusted advisor, particularly in matters of love, and along with God, was largely responsible for Grave's blooming relationship with Polly Loblolly.

He thought of Polly and wondered what she was doing. Probably out with Snoot or shopping on the boardwalk. He looked at his watch again. Or maybe a late lunch with Snoot. They had a thing about eating at Le Crabbe Bleu and he knew Polly would want to show Snoot her new crab-eating techniques. Grave, who was a long-time victim of her crab spray, was happy Salamander had come along and taught her how to properly disassemble a crab.

Crabs.

He was immediately hungry and restless. He looked over his shoulder again. Nothing. And then he turned to see Barry zooming up the path toward him. His flight had a sense of urgency. Barry was tilted forward, leaning into it, giving it everything he had to exceed the speed limit built into him.

He zoomed to a stop in front of Grave's face. "Sir, come quick, there's been a new development."

Here we go again, he thought. *Chasing our tails.*

"What now?" he said.

"God has found the source of the portal that killed the three women."

Grave stood up. "Where is it?"

"I don't know. Rum didn't say. He just wants us back at the station posthaste."

Grave looked in the direction where Salamander should be appearing, but there was nothing and no one. "Okay, stay here and wait for Salamander to get back. Then bring her along to the station."

"What's she doing?" said Barry.

"Trying to move the case along. She's talking to Van Hinkle, Dupree, and Denalia."

Barry chuckled mechanically, the period between each chuck less than ideal. "Ghosts again, sir? I thought you were over that?"

"No, seriously, that's who she's speaking to. Now wait, will you?"

"Whatever you say, sir."

"Good." Grave raced down the path to his Sprite, cranked it up, and sped away in the middle of a sound cloud, the gospel music impossibly growing louder the farther the car moved away from Barry.

Barry hovered by the bench, watching Grave go. "Ghosts," he said. "The man needs therapy, heavy-duty and soon."

60

Captain Morgan looked at his watch and compared its digital display to the clock on the wall. His conclusion: Grave was late and so was Salamander.

"Where are they?" he said.

And then they all heard the sound of gospel music, and couldn't help smiling. Seconds later, Grave burst into the conference room. "What is it?

Morgan pointed at a nearby chair. "Take a seat. Where's Salamander?"

Grave sat down. "At the cemetery. I left Barry behind to let her know to come as soon as she could."

"What were you doing at the cemetery? No, wait, don't tell me. Talking to a ghost. That little girl from the eighteenth century.

"Ghosts, actually," said Grave. "Victoria, yes, but also Van Hinkle, Dupree, and Denalia."

Morgan blinked. "What?"

"Yeah, Salamander is talking to the three of them, trying to get answers about their deaths and what the hell is going on with those cylinders."

"You know, it's one thing for you to talk to ghosts, Grave. We've all gotten used to your delusion, but Salamander? Really? You've got her talking to ghosts, too?"

Grave shook his head. He'd been through this ghost, no-ghost discussion many times, and he was tired of it. "Ghosts exist. Period. Now, can we get back to why we're here?"

Morgan shrugged and nodded at God. "Go on, Freeman."

God cleared his throat and looked around the table. "Our search of land, sea, and air around the bodies revealed just one hit closest to each of the bodies: a lighter-than-air vehicle." He looked down at his notes. "The LTA *Pegasus*."

"You mean a blimp?" said Grave.

"No, a zeppelin," said Snoot.

"No, a dirigible," said Loblolly.

"No, an airship," said Morgan.

"No, all four," said Smithers. "They're just different names for the same thing. All are airships."

"He's right," said Charlize.

"Okay," said Grave. "What do we know about it? Who owns it? Who flies it? Where is it?"

God held up a hand. "Slow down, slow down." He looked down at his notes again. "Right now, the *Pegasus* is assigned to aerial coverage of the tennis tournament."

Grave's eyes went wide. "I saw it, just the other day, at the country club. There were initials on it. ENI or INE or NEI."

"NEI, actually," said God. "For New Earth Industries."

"The NEI Blimp," said Morgan. "Last time I saw it was at the Super Bowl. Washington versus Berlin."

"Quite a game," said Blunt.

"Tell me about it," said Morgan.

"Stop," said Grave. "Let's stick to the point, shall we? Who owns New Earth Industries?"

God held up a finger. "Here's the interesting thing. It's owned by Koos Van Hinkle."

"Wow," said Grave. "We need to get over there and—"

Salamander burst into the room. "They were killed because they had second thoughts about the plan. They were going to go to the press."

Morgan rolled his eyes. "Don't tell me. The ghosts told you this."

"Exactly," said Salamander. "They were reluctant at first, but once Victoria explained to them that they were dead, they were more than cooperative."

"And whoever was on that blimp at the time is our killer," said Grave.

"It was Sloe Jim Phizz," said Salamander. "Or at least I think it was him. I didn't have a photograph to show them, but from their description of the man, I'd say it's Phizz. No doubt."

Grave turned to Morgan. "We need to get to that dirigible."

"Agreed," said Morgan. "And bring in Van Hinkle and all the others, just like we planned." He turned to Salamander. "And speaking of plans, what plan were those women talking about?"

"They were going to go somewhere, probably soon."

"Where?"

"Someplace called New Earth."

"New Earth?" said Morgan. He turned to God. "Do you have an address for New Earth?"

"No, not their corporate headquarters," said Salamander. "New Earth as in another *planet.*"

Morgan blinked. "Wow."

"Indeed," said Salamander.

"But in a zeppelin?" said Morgan.

Salamander sighed. "No, sir. In a portal cylinder, *inside* the blimp, I think."

"Oh, oh," said Morgan. "Then we need to get to that dirigible—fast. Grave, take Blunt and Salamander and find that blimp. If it's in the air, let me know, and I'll get some hoverchoppers to force it down. If not, take it over and arrest everyone aboard." He turned to God. "Release the Larrys. Send ten with Grave and take the rest of them with you to round up the others and bring them in."

"To the station?" said God.

"No, to C3, just as we planned. We need to be there to do the interviews—there's just more room—and besides, we need to be there to protect the cylinders."

Salamander shook her head. "Don't worry about the cylinders. I locked them down. They're not going anywhere—at least not in those cylinders."

"But there's probably a cylinder on the blimp," said Charlize.

"Right," said Morgan. He turned to Grave. "Why are you still here? Go find that dirigible and take down Phizz."

61

Grave turned off the Sprite's electric motor, and the gospel music faded away, replaced by the rising cheers coming from the tennis courts. He knew the final match had just ended and that they had little time before the crowd would be charging out, heading home.

He turned to Salamander and Blunt and ten very godlike looking Officer Larrys, who had already arrived. "Do you see the airship?"

Blunt pointed at the sky. "Up there, and already departing."

Grave looked around for Barry, who was just arriving. "Barry, get on the horn to Morgan. We need support to bring that blimp to the ground."

Barry said nothing, but lifted high into the air to make the call.

"Okay, everyone, let's see if we can find anyone on our target list. Salamander, take three officers and head to the left. Blunt, you take three officers and head to the right. I'll take the rest and go in through the main gate. Let's go!"

They moved away from the parking lot, executing Grave's orders, their heads on swivels looking for any of the persons of interest. Predictably, the crowds surged out, slowing the teams' progress. But after some minutes of forcing their way through the crowd, they made their way to the tennis court, where Viv Val was raising a trophy over her head.

Grave stopped in his tracks. All their targets were standing alongside her, smiling and applauding: Koos Van Hinkle, Heather's father, coach Larry Flan, tournament director Jacky Pompo, club director Manley Morris, concierge Sally Fifth, about twenty of Val's fellow competitors, and an equal number of male tennis players, who were apparently there to cheer Val on. A swarm of personal drones hovered and buzzed above them.

"Let's get them," said Grave, making his way through the last few spectators and leaping over a gate in the stands to make his way to the court. He could see Salamander's team and Blunt's team doing the same thing, surrounding everyone on the court.

Strangely, their targets didn't move, and instead of being terrified or showing any other emotion that might be remotely associated with apprehension by the police, they just laughed.

Grave shouted at them as he approached. "Don't move!"

And they didn't. There was simply a greenish-blue flash, and they were gone, people and drones together, leaving Grave's teams dumbstruck.

Grave looked up. No sign of the dirigible. He turned to Salamander. "What now? Where do you think they went?"

"They could be headed to NEI's landing pad across town, but I'm guessing—and it's only a guess—that they're headed back to C3 to make their getaway in that big cylinder."

"But you locked those cylinders down, right?"

"Right, so if we're quick about it, we can arrest them all at C3."

He turned to the others. "Okay, let's split up. Blunt, take your team to the NEI facility. If you see any evidence that they're there, give us a call."

"Right," said Blunt. He waved his arm in the air and shouted at his team. "Let's go!"

Grave gave his own command. "The rest of you, let's go!"

The sound of gospel music and police sirens soon filled the air.

62

Charlize and Smithers received the news first, as they sped along on the Third Intercoastal Highway, headed toward C3. "All right, Barry. We're already headed that way. No, I'll tell Morgan. You just keep following that blimp."

She looked in her rearview mirror. She could see Morgan's hovercruiser and the other police cruisers a few hundred yards behind her. "Smithers, get ahold of Morgan. Tell him the dirigible is on the way to C3. We'll get their first—there's no way they can keep up with our Duesenberg—but tell him to get there as quickly as possible."

Smithers nodded. "Right. On it."

Charlize nodded back and smashed her foot down on the accelerator, the Duesenberg nearly lifting off the ground.

Morgan watched Charlize and Smithers accelerating away. "Where in hell are they going?"

The call came seconds later.

"You're kidding me," said Morgan. "Okay, we'll try to catch up." He turned to Rum, who was resting on the seat next to the captain. "Tell everyone the airship is headed to C3. Everyone should converge there, stat."

Morgan pounded on the computer screen in front of him, trying to get the attention of the driving system. "Get a move on, we need to get to C3—fast!"

The computer responded after several seconds. "*Get a move on* is not a valid command. Please select your desires from the list to the right of the screen."

Morgan bellowed. "Stupid computer!"

Then he turned quickly to the list. "Um, um, um—here it is. "Faster, faster."

"Thank you for entering a valid command. Does this command apply to the current destination or do you want to reset your destination? Please respond from the list to the left of the screen."

"Same destination," Morgan screamed. "Same destination."

The computer came back on several seconds later. "That confirmation is not recognized. Please consult the list to the left of your screen."

Morgan rolled his eyes, and complied. "Um, um, um, okay. *Current destination confirmed.*"

"Thank you. Increased speed shall be applied in the direction of the current destination. Please set speed level."

Morgan growled at the computer screen. "As fast as you can go."

"I'm sorry, that is not a valid response. Please select a valid response from the list just below the computer screen."

Morgan had already turned three shades of red darker, but he managed to hold it together long enough to consult the list. "Um, um, um, okay. *Maximum speed.*"

"Thank you, said the computer. Now, shall we pass through traffic lights regardless of the signal color? Say YES for yes or No for no.

Morgan let loose a scream that would have made Grave's Sprite's gospel music sound like a whisper. "YES!"

The hovercruiser lurched forward, picking up speed, the world flying by in a blur.

The computer voice came back on. "Thank you. Please enjoy your ride."

63

Hovercopters and helidrones hovered over the C3 parking lot like they had something important to do, but all the important things had already happened. They had grounded the airship, which was now tethered to the ground on C3's expansive lawn, six Officer Larrys guarding it in stoic silence.

God had arrived first, just in time to see the passengers of the airship race across the lawn, up the building steps, and into the building. He had immediately established a perimeter, surrounding the building and stationing himself at the front door.

The others arrived almost simultaneously a few minutes later, Grave arriving last, the gospel music fighting with the roar of the helicopters for aural supremacy—and losing. He jumped out of the Sprite and raced up the steps of the building to join the others. "What's happening?"

Morgan turned to him. "Choppers forced them down, and they're now holed up inside. We've got the building surrounded, so they aren't going anywhere."

"What about those cylinders?" said Loblolly. "Can't they use those to escape?"

"No," said Salamander. "I locked them down. They'll need my key code."

"So . . ." said Loblolly.

"They're trapped," said Salamander.

"Sweet," said Snoot. "Let's go get them."

"Not so fast," said Morgan. "There may be a killer in there. We'll follow protocol." He turned to God. "You know what to do?"

God nodded. "I do. Officer Larrys first to prevent human injury or death. We'll take them down and then send for you."

"Be careful," said Morgan.

"God is always careful."

Morgan smiled. "Of course. So show me."

God waved to a group of Larrys and led them into the building, smashing open what was left of the already damaged front doors in the process. Morgan and the others could all hear shouts coming from deeper inside the building.

"They seem to be panicking," he said.

"Right," said Grave. "The fear of God is in them."

"Well, our God, anyway," said Morgan. He looked over at Salamander, who seemed to be distracted. "What's wrong?"

"The blimp. It has a portal device. I should go lock it down."

"No need. We have everyone trapped."

"Still, if things go sideways, they could make a run for the blimp and disappear."

Morgan nodded. "Fair point. Okay, go take care of it."

Salamander was already running toward the blimp. The sound of gunfire erupted behind her, coming from deep in the building.

64

Salamander was confused at first by the interior of the airship. There was no cylinder in evidence, just rows of seats with a small bar at the back. But then she saw a double door behind the bar. The cylinder would have to be behind those doors.

And it was.

She went into it, found the control panel, and locked it down by changing the key code. The interior of this cylinder seemed to be an exact replica of the portal device she had used on Mars, so she was pretty sure it was a short-distance model, not the kind that leaped from Mars to Earth in an instant.

Satisfied with her work, she raced back out of the dirigible, and ran to the C3 building. The mangled doors to the building were wide open and everything was quiet. She listened for a second more—nothing—then ran down the hall to Phizz's laboratory.

She stopped in her tracks when she entered the large room, which was now filled with her fellow detectives and a score of Officer Larrys. But there were no cylinders. They were gone.

Morgan heard her approach and spun around, frowning. "I thought you said you locked those cylinders down?" There was more than a little irritation in his voice. In fact, he was pissed.

"I did," she said. "Or at least I thought I did. There should have been no way for them to figure out my key code, let alone so quickly." She shook her head. "I don't understand."

She moved through the crowd and looked down at the space where the cylinders should have been. "This is just . . . impossible."

"And yet," said someone behind the others.

Salamander looked around to find the person who had spoken. "And yet what?"

"And yet they're gone," said the voice again.

"Who's speaking?" said Morgan. He'd never heard anyone on his team with a voice like that. It was high-pitched and scratchy, and more than a little creepy.

"Me," said the voice.

Everyone turned around, trying to find the person behind the voice. Morgan and Salamander moved through them until they came to one of the workbenches in the lab. A tennis ball and a plant sat in the center of the workbench.

"Where are you?" said Salamander.

"Right here," said the plant, lifting a frond and waving.

65

Everyone took a step back. A plant? A talking plant? And clearly not a plant from Earth. It was a bright bluish green, with circular leaves and a hexagonal stem that supported branches and a single triangular red flower.

Salamander took a step forward. "Who are you? What are you? And why are you here?"

"My name—my true name—is too long for your obvious impatience and too difficult to say given your rather basic voice boxes."

"So?"

The plant's single black eye looked around the room. "You can call me Lieutenant Press Here of the Mister Coffee Police Force."

"Um, okay," said Morgan. "What planet are we talking about?"

The plant looked around again. "Well, let's see now. Again, it's unpronounceable in your languages, so let's just say I come from Planet, um, Donuts."

Grave couldn't help chuckling. "Now that's a planet I'd like to visit."

The plant chuckled back, but the sound was less chuckle and more stepped-on cat. "No, you wouldn't want to do that. You'd meet the same fate as those misguided souls who just arrived there."

Morgan blinked. "They're on Planet Donuts?"

"Yes, and in custody, awaiting sentencing."

Morgan raised his eyebrows. "Really? How can we get them back? One of them committed three murders here."

"You can't. Besides, they will be summarily executed on the dark side of Planet Donuts within the hour, for the murders here, for my kidnapping, and for just showing up on our planet uninvited."

"That's incredibly fast," said Morgan.

"I think you have an expression here," said Press Here. "*Justice delayed is justice denied*, or some such."

"That's right," said Morgan. "But putting a person on trial takes time—selecting a jury, resolving motions, and so on."

Press Here chuckled again. "Trials? We have no trials."

"So just judges, huh?" said Morgan.

"Judges? No, no judges."

"Then what? Who?"

"We have the divine judgment of our leader." He paused to look around the room. "Let's call her Empress Exit."

"Um, okay," said Morgan.

Charlize stepped forward. "I'm curious about the location of your planet. You call it Planet Donuts, but we may have another name for it."

Press Here swayed back and forth. "All I can tell you is that we are a tidally locked planet. An eyeball planet, I think your scientists call it. We don't rotate, so half the planet is in light and half is in darkness at all times, just like your moon." He paused and cocked his flower. "Let's see what else can I tell you? Oh, we orbit a red dwarf star—let's not give it a name—and it takes about eleven of your earth days for one revolution around it."

Charlize nodded. "And would your planet be about 1.3 times the mass of Earth and 4.22 light years away?"

Press Here cocked his head again. "It would be. How did you know that?"

"Because it is the closest potentially habitable planet. We call it *Proxima b.*"

"That's a very strange name, but forgive me when I say that pretty much everything about your species is strange."

"Tell me about it," said Charlize. "I have to work with humans every day and sometimes they are behind comprehension." She paused and looked at the faces of the others in the room. "Um, sorry."

"Not a problem," said Morgan. "Let me ask you something, Press Here."

"Okay."

"Is there any chance we can at least get the cylinders back?"

"I wish that was a possibility. I mean, look at me, I'm stuck here. But no, Empress Exit has decided that Earth is not ready for the immense responsibility that comes with a machine that can traverse the universe in an instant. She fears you'd just blunder into interstellar space, causing havoc wherever you went."

Everyone nodded. A few started to speak, but didn't. Finally, Salamander took a step closer to Press Here. "I'm a bit confused about how they were able to escape in those cylinders. I locked them down. Changed the pass code."

Press Here nodded. "A simple answer. I unlocked each of them."

Salamander blinked. "But you're stuck in a pot."

Press Here looked down. "Oh, that." He stepped out of the pot and walked back and forth on what looked like feet made of roots. "I just walked into the cylinders, climbed to the instrument panel and made the change."

"But how could you know my code?"

Press Here shrugged. "I am a very smart plant. The chlorophyll is rich in me. A four-digit code is seed's play to me."

Salamander turned to Morgan and threw up her hands. "Well, I guess that's it."

And it was.

Epilogue

Polly Loblolly took a sip of her wine and shook her head. "Wow, quite a day."

Amanda Snoot was quick to react, rolling her eyes and almost spitting her wine into Loblolly's face. "You can say that again."

Loblolly looked around for the waiter, who was as invisible as usual, despite the fact that the outside dining area of Le Crabbe Bleu was nearly empty. "I mean, we were so close to getting them, and then . . ."

"Yeah, *poof*, gone."

"Salamander's fault, of course."

Snoot set down her glass. "How do you figure?"

"The key code, her key code. Who would think one-two-three-four was a safe code?"

Snoot nodded. "Yeah, but who would have expected that sentient plant from outer space?"

Loblolly chuckled. "I know." Her chuckle turned into an extended giggle. "Lieutenant Press Here." She slapped the table. "Hah!"

"We'll have to have a contest to rename him."

"Or her."

"Or it."

Loblolly shook her head. "No, I think Captain Morgan will have his way with that. He took the plant back to his office."

"I know," said Snoot, stifling a laugh. "I can't even begin to imagine the conversations they'll have."

"Right," said Loblolly. "And speaking of conversations, I bet our Captain Morgan is going to have a serious sit-down with Salamander. Everything turned out, like you said, but still, she royally screwed up. Just think what the world could have done with those cylinders."

"You've got a point."

"Of course I have. We could have explored thousands of exoplanets just like that." She tried to snap her fingers, but the wine had already removed that skill as a viable option. "Damn!"

Snoot saved her. "Ah, here comes the waiter."

Grave sat alone on the bench with Victoria, who had listened patiently to his retelling of the afternoon's events. "That's quite a story."

"Yeah, we almost had them."

"But it all worked out, except for the poor people who went to that planet. What did the plant call it?"

"Planet Donuts. Of course, it's really Proxima b, at least to us."

Victoria squinted at him. "Why are you really here, Simon? Something seems to be bothering you."

Grave sighed. "I was a little disappointed that the three women wouldn't talk to me, but they would talk to Salamander."

She shook her head. "That sigh tells me you were more than a little disappointed."

"I guess. No, you're right. Why wouldn't they talk to me?"

Victoria put a hand on his shoulder. "Simon, oh Simon, dear Simon, it wasn't you. They just felt more comfortable with a woman."

"You think?"

"I know. And you should feel lucky to have a young woman like Salamander on your side."

Grave chuckled sardonically. "For now."

"What? What do you mean?"

"She kind of screwed up with her ridiculous key code."

"Oh, Simon, don't blame her. She came up with the code on Mars where I bet there was little need for security."

"I understand that, but I don't think Captain Morgan is going to see it that way. Her stupid code led to the loss of a major technological achievement. Those cylinders were priceless."

Victoria sat up straight, alarmed. "Do you really think he'll punish her?"

Grave nodded. "I think so. As we were leaving, he gave her a stern look and asked her to come back to his office."

Victoria frowned. "Oh, dear."

Captain Morgan set Lieutenant Press Here down on the corner of his desk. "You can sit here for the moment." He turned to Salamander. "And you can sit down in that chair."

"Yes, sir." She sat down and watched as Morgan slumped down into his high-backed executive chair with a grunt.

"Quite a day, huh?" he said.

"Indeed."

"Not how I wanted it to turn out."

"Nor I."

He drummed his fingers on the desk. "The loss of those cylinders in incalculable."

She looked down. "I know, and I know it's my fault, and I know you won't put up with that."

Morgan grunted at her. "Normally, yes. *Normally*, I would already be escorting you to the Mars Terminal."

She cocked her head. "But, um, *abnormally?*"

He chuckled. "*Abnormally*, I would say our little friend here probably saved us from ourselves."

"Sir?"

"Just imagine the havoc we could cause in the universe with those portal devices. We'd infest the whole universe."

Salamander squinted at him. "I wouldn't go so far as *infest*."

"Well, I would, and that's the point. You made a mistake, yes, a stupidly simple key code, but this planet is better for it."

Salamander shook her head. "But—"

Morgan held up a hand. "No, just listen to me. I know you've got more than twenty-five days before you're scheduled to return to Mars, but—"

"You want me to leave now. Believe me, captain, I understand, and I'll—"

"Do no such thing. I want you here, on Earth, with us, *permanently*."

"What?"

"You may be young and a bit, well, *unusual*, but you're a damn fine detective, one I would be proud to work with."

Salamander leaped to her feet and extended her hand across the desk. "That would be wonderful, sir. *Wonderful!*"

Morgan shook her hand. "Now, find an empty desk out there and do your paperwork."

Salamander's smile seemed as big as Morgan's office. "Yes, sir. Yes, sir." She shook his hand again and raced from the office.

Morgan slumped back down in his chair, thoroughly satisfied. "That went well."

"Well for her, yeah," said Lieutenant Press Here, "but what about me?"

Morgan cocked his head. "Hmmm."

About the Author

Len Boswell is the author of eighteen additional books, including the award-winning *Simon Grave Mysteries*. He lives in the mountains of West Virginia with his wife, Ruth, and their dog, Daisy, a beagle who doubles as a paper shredder.

Note from Len Boswell

Word-of-mouth is crucial for any author to succeed. If you enjoyed *Simon Grave and the Girl with the Crab Tattoo*, please leave a review online—anywhere you are able. Even if it's just a sentence or two. It would make all the difference and would be very much appreciated.

Thanks!
Len Boswell

We hope you enjoyed reading this title from:

www.blackrosewriting.com

Subscribe to our mailing list – *The Rosevine* – and receive **FREE** books, daily
deals, and stay current with news about upcoming
releases and our hottest authors.
Scan the QR code below to sign up.

Already a subscriber? Please accept a sincere thank you for being a fan of
Black Rose Writing authors.

View other Black Rose Writing titles at
www.blackrosewriting.com/books and use promo code
PRINT to receive a **20% discount** when purchasing.

9 781685 134617